THE BROKEN ONE

THE ESCORT SERIES VOLUME 4

N.O. ONE

Warning / Foreword

Before you continue...
The Broken One is the fourth volume of a series of six.

It is graphic and morally on the fence, containing extremely sensitive material that may not be adapted to your needs. If you need specific details of things involved, please visit our website for a list of warnings.

www.author-no-one.com

If you're okay with all of this, just remember... we warned you.

On the plus side, the lead female is strong and proud and these men come with a fire extinguisher.

If you're still reading after all of that then, by all means, sit down, relax, and enjoy the filthy, bumpy road ahead.

To reiterate:

!! If you have triggers, please do not continue. This is not the series for you. !!

Seriously, if you don't want all the angst and smut with some suspenseful darkness thrown in for good measure, stop reading.

Did you stop?

No?

Excellent! You're now one of us and we have claimed you as our own, you filthy rebel you ;)

For everyone who feels broken, used up, at the end of their
tether...
You are worthy, you are important, you are fucking amazing.

CHAPTER ONE
RIVER

Standing on the front porch of Everest and Petal's home, I take in a deep, fortifying breath.

The whole way here, I wondered if I was doing the right thing, knowing damn well that Marco Mancini is a lot of things, but a quitter is not one of them. As soon as he realizes I'm gone, he'll have "his guy" looking for me.

Lifting my closed fist, I freeze right before making contact with the freshly painted door.

How long will it take Marco to figure out where I am?

My eyes instinctively dart to my raised hand and the missing rings from a very important finger. An image of Marco grinding his fucking molars as he finds the diamonds he placed on my finger flashes in my mind.

You know what? Fuck it.

That's what happens when you treat people like shit... they leave.

Before I can talk myself out of being here, I knock twice as my Rose mask slides on, ready to flash my award-winning smile.

"River! Oh my goddess, I'm so happy you're here!" Petal rushes me, wrapping her arms around my neck and squeezing like I haven't seen her in years.

"I got bored in that big mansion and needed some witchy love." Not a lie.

"Our home is your home, gorgeous." She turns as her fingers wrap around my wrist and she pulls me inside. "Literally."

We both laugh because she's not wrong.

"Ev, baby, look who's home!" Petal's voice is how I imagine a fae would sound echoing through the forest trees. If fae were real, that is.

I see his booted foot before anything else as he walks out of the kitchen and into the living room.

"Sister mine!" Fuck, I love this kid. My heart constricts with emotions, the need to seek comfort from my baby brother stronger than anything else.

Dropping my bag on the floor just to the right of the door, I rush Everest like he's an oxygen mask in the hazmat fire that is my life.

"Whoa, Riv! I'm not exactly stable with this thing." His arms are like a vice around my shoulders nonetheless. I'm sure I'm fucking with his balance, but, in this moment, I need to be selfish.

"Dude, what the fuck, man? Are you comin' or wh—"

My eyes pop open at the sound of Kai's voice just over Everest's shoulder.

"It's Sunday, we were just heading out for the market. Albeit late, but I'm moving slower these days. Fucking boot is a menace to my income." I laugh at Ev's grumpy complaint but don't release him for another couple of seconds, filling my lungs with the comfort of home.

"Sorry, I just missed you all. Do you need help?" Stepping back, I flex my coat-clad biceps to show them I'm capable of lifting a few boxes onto the truck bed.

"It's a man's job, Psyche." With a troublemaker's grin, he nods to the kitchen and tacks on, "You could fix us some grub though, for when we get home with the bacon."

"Eww, meat and sexism. Great combo. Now go away, Riv and I have catching up to do." Petal shoos them off, but not before she kisses her husband away.

Gah, I love my family.

Once everyone is gone and the silence of the house feels like a cement weight on my shoulders, Petal's face loses its fun-loving traits.

"Here, take these beads, you can help me while you tell me everything. *All* the details. And don't think I didn't notice your naked ring finger."

Crap, I should have known that nothing gets past Petal's superpower of observation.

I ignore her comment and we immediately get to work on her crafts. She makes candles and jewelry, both of her stations are buried under works in progress in the vast corner of her kitchen reserved just for this. As usual, we talk as we work.

I tell her very little and I have a feeling she knows I'm keeping shit from her. The problem is that anything I tell her would be difficult to explain without the context of our contract. It would be almost impossible to pour out my errant emotions without the truth of my profession. How am I supposed to explain that I just got fucked in the ass on the kitchen counter and dismissed like the employee I am? Which, in and of itself, isn't the end of the world except... it feels like it is. It's easy to forget you're a whore when you're treated like a goddess.

Until, that is, the proverbial bucket of ice water is thrown at your face, where you remember that getting fucked is literally in the contract and that emotions should be non-existent.

I can't tell her what I do, admit that I've been lying to them for the last eight years. The very idea of doing so makes me nauseous.

"Hmm, your aura is telling me a whole different story than you just having a tiff with Marco about kitchen appliances." Kissing me on the forehead, she gets up and lights a couple of candles sitting on the window ledge.

As soon as the scent reaches my nostrils, I choke and cough and almost panic as I look around the house, certain he's hiding somewhere in a dark corner.

"Vanilla, it's great for relaxation. It has a calming effect." The look on my face must tell her something is definitely wrong, and no amount of vanilla candles could make it right. "Are you okay? What's wrong?" Now she's looking around the house, probably trying to figure out what the hell is wrong with me.

"Nothing, it's fine. I didn't realize you were lighting candles."

"It's what I do. Heal by scent." She smiles, and when I take a good look at her, I realize she's being a bit facetious. My gaze runs over her features and yep, there it is.

"You did it on purpose." The little minx.

"I have no idea what you're talking about." With a self-satisfied grin on her pretty face, she sits back down next to me and waits.

I stare at her, knowing damn well she wants the whole story. One I cannot tell her.

"Petal."

"River."

Fucking hell, my family is nosy.

"Fine. Marco and I got into a fight." I'm hoping it's enough to satisfy her curiosity.

"No kidding. Your aura is so dark right now, I'm thinking we need to surround you with some green to shift it back. Have you been eating healthy? Sometimes going back to your roots can help your aura fade back to your natural color."

"Yeah, remember Luca, our chef? He feeds me like a queen."

We both get a faraway look in our eyes. No doubt Petal is recalling the exquisite meals we'd been served while they were there with me. He even paid special attention to making sure we were all fed with organic food, and made some new vegan creations for Ev and Petal.

"Right, so this dark cloud has something to do with Marco."

"Yes." It's all I give her and she accepts it.

For now.

Just as I hear my brother's booming laughter outside, I look up at the cuckoo clock above the kitchen table and realize more than four hours have passed. We haven't even made lunch yet.

"Babe! We need some vinegar and dish soap mix. A whole fucking lot of it too."

Petal and I look at each other and at the same time, we realize what's happening.

"Skunk." We say it in unison as Ev comes wobbling up the back porch steps, his face screwed up like he's just sunk his teeth into a lemon.

The smell is overwhelming as I step outside and watch Kai run to the hose after securing what little is left from the market.

"What happened?" I'm covering my face to avoid inhaling the invading smell of the animal's spray.

"Fucker came out of nowhere. I tried to swerve and hit the brakes pretty hard to avoid it all together, but he just froze in the middle of the fucking road and let her rip once we were right above it." Ev hobbles back outside and throws the mix to Kai, who catches like a pro baseball player. Covering his face with his bandana, he squats and sprays the undercarriage and the tires until there's nothing left in the bottle.

"He got us good. It's like he sat there under the truck and emptied himself out." Ev fills up another bottle and throws it to Kai.

"Poor little guy, you scared him to death." Petal's face contorts in pain for a brief second before she asks. "Did you kill him?"

"No, babe. Chill. He flew out of there like a bat out of Hell."

We all visibly relax.

Once it's safe to approach, we all step down and join Kai as he hoses down the truck completely.

It's freezing outside, but there's something comforting about helping your family pull together. Petal recoups the bottles as Ev throws the tarp off his vegetables in the back.

Without hesitating, I jump up on the bed of the truck and pass down the crates to Kai, who's handed the hose to Everest.

"How'd it go today?" There's barely anything left here.

"Great. Had a big family come in and load up for the month. It's soup season, after all."

Perfect time to store and use as needed.

Just as I'm about to jump off the bed, Kai holds up his arms and grabs me by the waist to help me down. Over his shoulder I see two things simultaneously.

First, Freya pulls up right behind Kai. Second, and a little more troubling, if not outright irritating, is the sleek, red Aston Martin parked along the curb.

I know that car.

I've had orgasms in that fucking car.

As my feet hit the ground, my eyes bore into the figure leaning against the hood, his imposing stature making my entire body hum with both anger and desire.

"*Tesoro*, looks like you're having a good time."

Fucking Marco Mancini and his control issues.

CHAPTER TWO

RIVER

"**H**ow are you here?"

Kai's grip leaves my waist as I move away, feeling total déjà-vu as I head toward Marco.

"You're smarter than that, *Tesoro*. I know you can see the car behind me." He's smirking, but the air around him is smothered in anger. A growl reverberates through his chest as his steel-gray eyes flick over my shoulder.

"You know what I mean. Don't be an asshole. How did you find me so quickly?" We're toe-to-toe now, my hands on my hips, and I can hear Petal whisper-yelling at the guys to stay away, to let me deal with it.

"I know where you are at all times." He raises a brow, only adding to the sexy-as-fuck look on his stupid fucking face. I want to smack it off of him.

"Stop being so cryptic. How the fuck do you know where I am at all times?" Had he followed me, he would have been here hours ago. Although, thinking about it, he got rid of my apartment months ago, and I'm positive he doesn't know about my work apartment, so this is the logical option. Fuck. Why am I so predictable?

"Your phone." He follows this sentence with a shrug of his shoulders. *What does my phone have to do with it?*

My mind is reeling, trying to add up all the morsels of information he's leaving at my feet, when it dawns on me...

"You've been fucking tracking me?" I back off slightly in horror at my realization. I knew he was a possessive asshole, but he's been *tracking* my phone?

"Clever girl. And I'm sure I've asked you not to use those foul words in public. That filthy mouth is mine." One step forward, and he's reduced the small space I just put between us.

"You can ask all you fucking like, Marco. But I am not yours to command. Don't you understand how fucked up all this is?" My voice is raised, and I have no doubt the others can hear me, but right now, I'm seeing red.

Marco has gone too far, once again, and it's time I put a stop to it. Too much of myself has been lost with this contract. I've broken my own rules and allowed more than I ever should have.

"I need to keep you safe. This is the only way. But you're wrong about one thing... you *are* mine." His deep-gray eyes get impossibly darker, and it's like we have some weird stare-off going on. Neither one of us is willing to back down.

"Well, not anymore. I can take care of myself. I'm done, it's over." I'm trying to be cryptic, so my family won't ask too many questions about what's going on when this fucker eventually leaves. Because he will leave, he can't stay here.

"Oh, *Tesoro*." He leans down, his face level with mine. "With us, it is *never* over."

"Fuck off, Marco. This is not the time or place for your macho bullshit. Go home." I turn to walk away, but before I can take a step, Marco grips my arm, twisting me back to face him.

"No. I won't allow you to choose him."

"Kai is and will always be my best friend. You ca—"

"You have it all wrong, *Tesoro*. I'm talking about Nathaniel." Marco's scowl is serious, no hint of a smirk anymore.

"Why is Nathaniel relevant here?" Jealous asshole. He sees one interaction and assumes the worst. I suppose Marco Mancini and Nathaniel Reed have a lot more in common than I first thought.

"I saw the way he looked at you, and I know you used to date him."

"And why is that any of your business? I didn't do anything that could tarnish your reputation. I had a simple conversation with a man at a party. Nothing more, nothing less."

"*Tesoro*, he's not who you think he is."

"Oh, really? Would you care to enlighten me? Expand on that ridiculously vague sentence? Because I think you're a jealous asshole with control issues, and you're talking shit."

I've pushed my boundaries constantly with Marco, but right now, he looks about ready to snap. His usual anger bubbling under the surface is showing with his heavy breaths, deep growls, and narrowing eyes. It should scare the fuck out of me, that this man boiling over with rage has a vice-like grip on my arms, holding me in place, but it doesn't. Even after the rough ass-fuck this morning, I know he won't hurt me like Frank did.

"You need to stay away from him." The words are spoken through clenched teeth in a deep, barely-controlled voice.

"No. I can do whatever the fuck I want, Marco. And if Nathaniel is one of those things, you've got no fucking say in that."

"Wrong again, *Tesoro*. We have a contract." He's raising his voice now, which I could really do without. Listening ears behind me and all that.

"Screw your fucking contract. You don't get to treat me like a goddamn whore and expect me to come running when you snap your fingers. Those were not the terms of our agreement. I have returned all of your dirty money too. So it's done. You have no say in anything I do any longer." I'm whisper-yelling, speaking through gritted teeth so the conversation stays between us, and I'm on a roll, unable to stop the words spewing from my mouth. "And lastly, Nathaniel never made me fucking kill someone. So you'll have to forgive me, or not, but I kind of have a lot more trust in him than I do for you."

"Better you kill someone than someone killing you."

"Stop with all your cryptic bullshit, Marco. I'm done. I've had enough. I cannot do this"—I gesture between us as best I can with my arms trapped in his hold—"any more."

"You clearly need some time. I'm a generous man, I can give you that. But let's be clear about one thing. Your safety has always been—and will always be—my priority."

"Oh, fuck off. Seriously."

He surprises me by pulling me impossibly closer, letting go of my arm in favor of gripping my chin and planting his lips on mine for a soul-stealing kiss, our tongues warring with each other in a dance for dominance.

As he pulls away, we're both panting for breath, but he turns and walks back to his car. Leaving me standing, staring dumbfounded at the whole interaction, and before he opens the car door, he pauses and looks back to me.

"You can keep the money, you earned it. Forget the contract. But in the eyes of the law and my family, you are still my wife, and I trust you will respect that. See you soon, *Tesoro*."

With that, he climbs into his ridiculously pretentious car and drives off. Leaving me confused as fuck.

Why show up just to cause shit? And I never did get a straight answer about him tracking me. *Asshole*. Why is it that after an argument, you always think of much better things to say?

It's when I turn toward the house that I realize I'm a whole lot closer to the front porch than I anticipated. And they've just witnessed this whole interaction in stunned silence.

I hold my breath as I look at my family, those who have always been there, my safe space, and I hope to fuck they don't realize exactly what was being discussed. But the looks on each of their faces are ones of disappointment.

"I knew it."

"Shut the fuck up, Freya."

At least Kai still has my back?

Chapter Three

River

"Riv, what was that?" Surprisingly, Ev is first to speak, his voice full of wary curiosity.

"It's nothing for you to worry about. I mean, Marco and I are obviously over, so it looks like I'm about to become a divorcée." I'm trying to play this off with a little humor as I shrug my shoulders, hoping to all the gods that they didn't hear the whole conversation between Marco and me.

"So it's perfectly normal to have a contract and get paid by your husband?"

I wish I could smack the smug grin off of Freya's face, and I'm a little sad that Kai hasn't told her to shut the fuck up again, but I can still play this off as nothing. I think.

"Have you ever read Fifty Shades, Freya?"

The smug grin doesn't disappear, in fact, it grows... as do Petal's wide eyes and Ev's scowl. Kai is the only one who seems like he wants to believe me, but he remains silent. Speechless.

"Was Freya right when she called you an escort? Is that what this is, Riv?" Ev's voice is low, deep, disbelieving. And it's breaking my heart.

"I fucking knew it. I told you she wasn't so innocent, Kai. Now you have to believe me." Freya is clinging to Kai's arm like he's her very reason for breathing.

"Freya, stop. Please go home. I'd like to talk with my sister-in-law without your negative energy surrounding the situation." Petal looks a little angry, her doll-like features screwed up and serious. I don't like it, it's not natural for her. Not to mention, in Petal-speak, she basically just told Freya she's a cunt and to fuck off out of her house.

"I'll take her home, Pet." Before turning to leave with the bitch formally known as my friend, Kai approaches me, a hand on each of my cheeks as he looks me straight in the eye. "You and me, we need to find some time to talk. No more bullshit. Okay?"

I slowly nod as he releases my face, but not before he shakes his head and plants a gentle kiss on my forehead. He walks away without glancing back, Freya following behind him like a lost puppy who has found their master. He's mad, the sadness in his eyes as he looked at me in that moment speaks of disappointment, the same kind I can feel coming from Ev and Petal.

Will I ever get a respite from all the drama and shit? Though, I suppose I've made my own bed, it's time I lie in it.

"Can we go in and sit? We can talk, and I'll explain everything."

"I want the truth this time, Riv. I don't know how long you've been lying to us, but it's not okay. I'm your brother, for fuck sake. Since when did lying to your family become normal?"

"Come on, Bear. Let's head inside and take a breath." Petal strokes her hands down Ev's back and arm as she gently guides him into the house, a quick look of pity in my direction as they walk through the front door.

With a deep breath, I steel my spine and prepare myself for this mental torture I'm about to endure. This is all of my own doing. I have no one to blame but myself, and while I'm not ashamed of my lifestyle, I'm ashamed of the lies I've had to tell.

Joining Ev and Petal in the living room, I sit on the chair opposite the couch, face to face with two of the people who mean the most to me in the world. Petal's features are full of worry and sadness, her arm resting over Ev's shoulders in comfort. He's a sensitive soul at heart, and I can only imagine the thoughts running through his mind at this revelation.

Not that I've outright admitted it yet, but it's out there now. I need to come clean, pull up my big girl panties and explain myself.

Ev's pissed at me, I can feel it coming off him in waves, see it in his face as he grinds his jaw, his eyes on me and full of disappointment.

"Are you going to tell us what's going on then, or are we going to sit here all day staring at each other?"

"Ev, baby, calm down. Give her a chance to explain." Petal looks to me next. "Please, Gorgeous. Tell us what's going on. The truth." Her tone is soft and wistful, but there's a hardness to it, telling me she's holding it together for her husband.

There's no easy way to tell them. No way to dance around the truth, so I close my eyes, take another deep breath, and let it all out.

"Yes, Freya is right. I'm not officially a life coach, I'm an escort. I have been since a few months after Mom and Dad died. I—"

"Do you have any idea how dangerous that is, Riv? And in Manhattan? For fuck sake, it's surprising they haven't found you by the side of the road in a body-bag at this point."

"Don't be dramatic, Ev. I haven't been frequenting street corners and going off to have sex with complete strangers." Well, technically, I only know them on paper, but I'm not digging a deeper hole for myself.

"Oh, so you know all the people who have been paying you for sex?"

"Not exactly. Bu—"

"So you *are* fucking strangers."

"Calm down, Bear. Let her speak." Petal's voice calms him a little, but he's still bubbling inside.

"Look, it's not that bad. I've been safe, I promise. There is always a contract in place, after a huge amount of re-search. It's not always about sex either. Sometimes they just want the company, someone to talk to who won't judge them."

"That's what a psychiatrist is for, Riv, not a fucking prostitute."

"Ev, I know you're pissed, but watch your language. There's no need to be so rude, I raised you better than that."

"I'm not sorry. Don't forget, we know all about the attacks. The shit that's been going on with you lately is all because of this fucking job. I don't give a shit that you have sex for money. But what I do give a shit about is you putting yourself in these dangerous situations. Riv, I could've lost you too and I'm not okay with that." The anger Ev has been emitting has subsided, and is now being replaced by pure sadness and concern for my safety. Petal continues to rub soothing circles over his back with her palm, her other hand resting on his twitching thigh.

"I get it, I really do. And I am sorry that I've kept this from you, but at the time, it was all I could do to take care of us. Mom and Dad were gone, and I had to find a way to prove I was responsible enough to keep you with me. You were only thirteen, they could have taken you away to a foster ho—"

"Don't give me all that, Ginny and Brad were there. They wouldn't have allowed that and you know it."

"While that is partially true, I needed a way to provide for us without relying on other people. You were still *my* responsibility. I couldn't bear for you to miss out on a single thing, and I did what I had to so we could eat. But it allowed so much more than that; you were able to do anything you wanted, your options were endless, and every time I saw you smile when I could provide that for you..." I sigh, remembering Everest's cute little face the first time

I was able to take him shopping without watching what we were spending. "It just made my heart so happy, Ev. I wanted to be able to put that smile on your face every day. And then when you grew up and wanted to go to college, I could do that for you. I felt like a proud parent seeing their child fulfill all their dreams."

While I'm speaking, a tear forms in Petal's beautiful big brown eyes, like she understands what I've done for them both. Ev, on the other hand, deflates. As if all his energy has been zapped away at my honesty.

"Riv, you're not my parent though. You shouldn't have put yourself in danger like you have for me. We're supposed to be a team, we work together. You've done so much for us, and you know I could never thank you enough for that, but if I'd known how much you were truly sacrificing... I don't think I could have accepted it. Your safety doesn't come before my happiness and I'm so pissed at you right now." He places his head in his hands, and Petal's tears slowly creep down her face.

I hate that I've done this to them. Seeing my brother like this is the last thing I ever wanted.

"Ev, I—"

"Don't." I can barely hear him, but his broken voice speaks volumes.

"Bear, just let her finish. Please. Go on, Beautiful."

Even though she's upset, she's not angry. Her voice is calm and soothing as always, her empathetic nature ever present. She feels everything we're all going through with this, understanding every angle, and she's like a shining light in an endless storm.

Ev looks up at me, his elbows on his knees and his shoulders slumped in defeat as he waits for me to complete my explanation.

I go into detail about the contracts, the research I do before taking on a client, how much Polly helped me in the early days. They remain silent the whole time, allowing me to talk about my secret life for the last eight years. Petal nods in understanding, all the while clinging to her husband with loving arms.

"So what about Marco? Why is he different? You have all these rules, yet I'm pretty sure you've broken them all for him." Petal is inquisitive, not judging, and the small tip of her lip in a knowing smile tells me she has her own theories on this.

"It has a lot to do with Nathaniel, Mr. Bobby, and you guys. I was offered an opportunity to take over Polly's businesses, and I thought I could do it. Start a new chapter of my life where the control is all mine again, unafraid of secrets and deceit. I wouldn't have to lie to you anymore, I could have a normal boyfriend. Marco came along at the right time and he was supposed to be my last client."

"Hmm." Petal raises a brow in disbelief.

"Sounds like a cheesy movie where the cop about to retire takes on one last job and fucking dies." Ev's voice is raspy, deep, full of hurt. "I get it, Riv. You're a fucking superwoman who feels like she needs to take the whole world on her shoulders. I admire you for that, but I'm not going to pretend it doesn't hurt like fuck. I'm going outside for a joint. Don't follow me, Riv." Turning to give Petal a sweet kiss, Ev then stands and walks—booted foot and all—to the back patio doors.

"Ev, do you want me to leave? Give you ti—"

"Why would you leave, Riv? It's your fucking house, isn't it?" With that, he slides open the door and goes outside.

Looking to the floor, I sigh, placing my head in my hands.

With gentle footsteps, Petal approaches and strokes my hair back away from my face. "He's hurting. Give him some time to process. You know what he's like."

"Yeah, I know. I'm sorry, Pet." I stand and look her in the eyes, taking another deep breath before wrapping my arms around her. She returns it with all her might, and it sends a warmth through me that only family can provide. I allow my tears to trickle down my cheeks at the comfort this wonderful tiny woman gives me.

"Thank you for being honest with us, Beautiful. I know it must have been hard. But please understand, all we've ever wanted was for you to be happy and safe. What are you going to do now?" She pulls away and holds my arms, staring into my soul to sense the truth of my next words.

"Honestly, I have no idea, Pet."

How could I possibly answer her question when my entire world has just blown up in my face faster than a Mets game?

My life is in a million pieces.

My family is shattered and hurting.

And me? Well, that's simple.

I'm just broken.

Chapter Four

Marco

River Fox infuriates me. Why must she be so diffi-cult? She could have the whole of New York City at her feet, doing her bidding, but she refuses to play by my rules. Instead, here I am playing by *her* fucking rules and I don't like it.

I am a man of action.

For any given situation, I assess the problem, find possible options, and execute the solution. My entire life has been this simple because I have the means to make sure my family and my business are safe.

Whether she likes it or not, River is now my family and I protect what's mine. Except, me sitting here in this car is probably the most ridiculous solution I've ever come up with. Enzo is on the other side of the street making sure there are no threats to my wife. I'm guessing he'd rather be anywhere but here—probably somewhere in the vicinity of my sister and pretending I don't know about it—but tough shit. I need him to be the eyes in the back of my head at all times.

For the last hour, I've watched River settle into her apartment. For some reason, this place wasn't on our radar and I made sure Stefano understood how unacceptable that oversight was for me. Without moving from the car—I borrowed Stefano's so River couldn't identify me since the Aston was a bit too conspicuous—I know every step she takes.

Coffee shop.

Grocery shopping.

Some witchy store that sells two-dollar necklaces. I can give her diamonds and rubies all day long, but she wants fucking crystals.

Duly noted, Tesoro.

As insane as it sounds for me to be here, I have this deep-rooted feeling in my gut that something's not right. That danger is still lurking in the dark corners of the city and it's got River in its sights.

I die and kill for my family.

For River, I would incinerate the whole fucking city and watch her rise from the ashes. So, if stalking her to make sure she's safe is unbecoming, then I guess I'm as hideous as they come.

Looking down at my phone, I see the tracker stopping at the grocery store. Again.

Scrolling until I find Enzo's name, I tap on the call button and am grateful that he doesn't make me wait before he answers.

"Yeah."

"She's back at the store." I'm surprised my molars haven't lost half an inch from all the grinding I do, day in and day out, since River bulldozed into my life.

"I know."

"I need to go see if she's okay." He could be there, luring her back into his world and I would be none the wiser.

"And then what?"

"What do you mean, and then what? Then I take her back to her place. Carry her over my fucking shoulder like a fireman if I have to. What the fuck kind of question is that, Enzo?" Every fiber in my body tells me I need to protect her.

"Yeah, that'll win her over. Great plan, boss. You should run for office." Any other day I'd laugh at his bluntness. Today, though? I want to punch his honesty in the face.

"Okay, smart ass. What do you suggest?"

"I suggest you look behind you." My head spins so fast I risk whiplash. At the sight of her carrying a paper bag with what I know is wine from the way she's holding the neck, my entire body relaxes. It's like seeing her sends relief throughout every muscle, making it easier to breathe.

I was half sure she'd come back with Candy Aisle Guy.

Yeah, I know about the nickname River gave Nathaniel. He was proud of it. I know this because he told us.

"She's alone." It's not a question, obviously, since I can see it with my own eyes. Yet, I need to vocalize it so that it becomes true.

"No shit, boss. If I were you, I'd run down to that flower shop up on thirty-second and get her something nice." This guy who is capable of making people talk when they refuse to give us information is—deep down in his cold-blooded heart—a romantic.

As soon as River disappears through her low-level security building, which is another reason I grind my fucking teeth all day long, I hop out of my car and follow Enzo's advice.

Before I even make it down the street, my phone rings, Lina's name flashing on my screen. I debate sending her to voicemail, but then I remember she's my sister and stubbornness runs in the family.

Fourteen generations back.

"Mancini."

"You sound just like Dad. It's concerning." I smile, her words making me proud despite the tone.

"What can I do for you, Little Sister? Make it quick, I'm busy." Turning the corner, my eyes land on the colorful sign hanging just above the door—"Nympheas Flower Shop"—and I chuckle, knowing damn well the name would make River smile.

Fuck, I've gone too soft when it comes to her.

Since when do I back down? Or negotiate? That's not me.

Yet, as my hand reaches out for the door knob, compromising with River seems like the most natural thing in the world.

"I hope you're busy getting our girl back. How did you manage to fuck up so bad that your wife is gone barely a month after she said 'I do'?" And the grinding continues.

"Language, Lina. I may not be Dad, but I will take away your allowance." As if she cares.

"Just in case you don't hear me, I'm rolling my eyes at you right now."

"And so we're clear, River isn't gone. She's..." The little bell inside the shop rings out loud enough to make me growl. "Visiting family."

"Welcome to Nympheas, can I help you?" I was expecting a cheerful vendor ready to sell me the entire store, but what I get is a cranky teenager barely able to lift her face from her phone to acknowledge my presence.

"You're so full of shit, I can smell it from the penthouse." Spoiled brat.

"What do you need, Lina?"

"I need you to give my body guards the day off. They won't listen to me and I want some girl time today." This makes me pause for a second.

"I don't see how one is incompatible with the other." My index finger caresses a ruby-red rose petal, reminding me of River's smooth skin as my tongue learned every nook and crevice of her body.

"I'm not going to the spa with two gorillas watching at the front door. It's embarrassing." She sounds like she did when she was fourteen and pretending to be thirty.

"There's too much going on right now. Too many variables to just let you go rogue." Leaning down, I take a deep inhale of a large white flower with a yellow stem poking out.

"You're impossible. I'm not the President's daughter, Marco. I don't see why I can't move about freely. This is ridiculous." I don't need to see her to know she's pouting.

"No, you're not. You're a Mancini, and that's worth more than any President of any country."

"Whatever, I need some privacy, Marco. Make it happen, please." Now, she's using her five-year-old voice, making sure the last syllable drags on for a mile. "I promise I'll be careful. Oh, and I'll make you the spinach lasagna you love so much that Luca refuses to make."

Rolling my eyes as I grab the biggest bouquet of roses—red, of course—in the whole damn shop, I know I'm going to concede to my sister before the words even come out of my mouth.

"Fine, but I want updates to make sure you're all good. Is that clear?" Nodding to the vendor behind the wooden table that serves as a counter, I reach into the inside pocket of my coat and take out my wallet.

"Gah, you're a pain in my—"

"Do not finish that sentence, Lina. I swear, River is a terrible influence." I mumble the last sentiment, telling myself that the small grin on my lips is just a muscle reaction to the overwhelming scents in the flower shop.

"Funny, she's a great influence on you. It looks good on you, you know?" I freeze. My brow slanted in confusion as I hand my credit card to the young woman in front of me.

"What are you talking about?"

"Love. It suits you."

By the time I'm back at River's place, Enzo gives me the lowdown on who came and went into the apartment building.

"Lady with her chihuahua, kid coming home from school, couple of delivery guys. Nothing suspicious." I swear, this guy does not ever waste a single breath.

"Okay, I'm going up."

"'Bout fucking time."

"*Muto!*" He may not talk much on a good day, but I don't need him saying any more.

Because I only found out about this apartment recently, I have to wait for someone to go in and charm my way behind them.

"That's quite the bouquet you've got there, young man." I flash my signature Mancini smile that I've perfected throughout the years for situations just like these. "In my experience, that size means one of two things: you're either in the dog house or you're proposing."

He's not wrong. I hold up my left hand, showing off my wedding band and shrug to acknowledge my guilt.

"Doghouse it is, then. Good luck, son."

"Thank you, sir."

I'm not sure which apartment is hers, all I know is that she's on the third floor since I saw her moving around at her window this morning. As I reach her landing, I'm faced with three closed doors. From the layout of the building, the right door makes the most sense and without hesitation, I march forward and firmly knock twice.

"Coming!"

I grin at her response, the words, "Soon, *Tesoro,*" itching to ring out, but I hold myself back, hoping the red roses go a long way to convincing her to let me in.

If not, I'll do what I usually do.

Impose.

"Hey, sorry, I was just—" With the arrangement taking center stage, I grin when she suddenly stops talking. She may not be able to see my face, but I have no doubts she knows exactly who I am.

"You got the wrong apartment, buddy. Mrs. D'Amato is next door."

Lowering the flowers, I pin her with my stare. Of all the women in my life, River Fox—no, River Mancini—is the only one who doesn't cower.

"Actually, I'm looking for Mrs. Mancini." Raising my brow, I grace her with my typical smirk.

"I hear she hangs out in the Hamptons. You should try her there."

"Cute."

"Not cute. Truth."

With one step I'm invading her space, the sweet scent of her perfume making me weak in all the right places.

"*Tesoro*, let me in. We need to talk."

"Trust me, you've said enough. I'm good." Fucking hell, she's the fire to the fuel that runs through my veins.

"At least, allow me to apologize." The word is like acid on my tongue but desperate times and all that shit.

River laughs outright, like saying I'm sorry is out of my depth.

"I got you roses, you should put them in a vase." I take another step, forcing her to walk backward, and that's when it hits me.

The sickly-sweet smell of paint.

"You can't come in here like you own the place, Marco. I told you, this contract is done."

"You did and you're right. The contract is null and void." I watch her facial expression as I give her the news, hoping and even praying she'll have a reaction.

Regret.

Sadness.

Despair.

Instead, I'm greeted with that fucking mask she wears so well and, in that moment, I want to grab her by the throat and fuck the indifference right out of her.

"Good. I'll take your roses as your white flag and let you get on your way."

By the time she's finished with her sentence, roses firmly in her grasp, I'm inside her tiny apartment, my coat hanging on top of the nearest chair.

"What are you doing?" Without a word, I scan her living room.

"It occurs to me that as your *husband*, I should be here to help you freshen up." Folding one sleeve up, then the other, I swing my gaze to meet her fire dead on.

"You need to leave."

"That would be rude of me. We can't have that."

"Marco, you just said we were done. I can handle this on my own, thank you very much." Too much talking, not enough action.

"No, I said our contract is done. Our marriage, *Tesoro*, is very much alive." Her windows and doors are ready for the first coat of paint. "I see you've already taped off the edges. This should be quick."

"We need to divorce then." I almost scoff at her words. She's so strong but she doesn't realize the danger she's in either. I may be stalking her, but I'm not the only one. And if I tell her what's going on, I'm afraid she'll do something stupid that'll accelerate the entire plan.

So, for right now, all I can do is be the obstacle that keeps her alive.

"If you moved a little faster, this job would be done in no time. So, the fact you're holding us up tells me you're hoping I stay the night." Unable to keep my hands to myself any longer, I wrap my fingers around her throat and squeeze just enough to see her pupils dilate, feel her breath hitch and her body relax into my touch. "But, *Tesoro*, all you need to do is ask and I'll be here. Better yet..." Running my nose up the side of her jaw, I whisper into her ear. "I'll take you home and punish you until you come on my tongue, my fingers, and my dick."

To my satisfaction, her body betrays her with a small moan that makes my dick harder than steel.

"Why are you here?" The venom in her words is just under the surface of her lust.

"I'm always here for you, River."

"You're infuriating."

I'm expecting her to push me away, put up a fight. Scream and kick.

What I don't expect is her lips slamming into mine. Our tongues warring out our frustrations, our bodies working from muscle memory. It's barely been twenty-four hours since I last felt the hot, welcoming sheath of her cunt around my cock, but it feels like a lifetime.

By making the first move, she has opened up the gates of my need and only a divine intervention could pry me away from her.

My free hand flies straight to her nape, grabbing onto her hair and pulling her head back enough so that I can devour her mouth. Neither one of us is holding back as we seek each other out, biting and sucking and licking every inch we can find.

"Oh, *Tesoro*, it's what you love most about me." Spinning her around, I slam her against the nearest wall as I kick the painting supplies out of my way, too eager to take what's mine.

"No, it's what I hate about you."

Lies. Every word. And she damn well knows it.

Just as her head bangs against the wall, I strip her naked below the waist before sinking to my knees so the first thing I see and smell is the perfection that is her pussy. There's no hesitation on her part, legs spreading wide enough for me to pull her thigh over my shoulder and bury my tongue in her sweet cunt, lapping up every ounce she gives me.

"Your dripping pussy is telling me a whole different story."

With her fingers fisting my hair, I'm almost distracted by the pain she's giving me. The punishment she's doling out. The control she's demanding from me.

"That's just physical, any tongue could make me wet. It has nothing to do with you." If I hadn't fucked her ass raw the day before, I'd strap her to that St. Andrew's Cross and spank the truth out of her gorgeous mouth. She's no doubt sore and I'm not a complete dick.

I'm making no promises for next time, though.

But right now, my only thought is to feast on her, drink down her intoxicating cum, make it a part of me.

In fact, my only concern is making her lose her ever loving mind, then doing it all over again until her knees give out.

Her thighs are trembling with every effort she makes to stay standing, her muscles moving against my palms just as the tip of my tongue finds her clit—hard and proud—needing my attention like nothing else.

Every moan that escapes River's parted lips encourages me to suck harder, to force the orgasm from her body and remind her that I own her. Her pleasure. Her needs. Every fucking one of her orgasms are mine.

'Till death do us fucking part.

"Fuck!" There it is, her need is building, her climax coming to fruition, and I'm at its door ready to reap my reward.

Without thinking, I add two fingers in one swift thrust up her hot, throbbing pussy before curling the ends and sucking on her clit, hard. Harder than ever.

"Goddammit!"

I don't let her go. In fact, I fuck her even harder with my fingers and my tongue. My entire body is working to make her lose every ounce of control she tries to hang on to. I need her to know that I'm her rock. I'm the pillar she can rest upon. I'm the only man capable of giving her the good and bad at the exact moment she needs it.

"Give it to me, *Tesoro*. Let it go."

And she does.

It's beautiful and tragic. It's a hurricane and a tornado. It's deafening screams and convulsing limbs.

Her orgasm is as beautiful as her soul. Pure and strong.

And I'm the man who gets to eat it all up.

Once we've both regained control of our ragged breaths, I sit back on my haunches and place her leg back in place. She's still naked from the waist down and I hate to think of her covering any part of her body.

"You said you didn't get down on your knees for any-one." Raising my head to look her dead in the eyes, I allow a genuine smile to grace my mouth—lips glistening with her juices—before licking up every drop of her orgasm.

"I make an exception for my wife."

"Well, your *fake* wife is tired and you, sir, can get the fuck out of my apartment. Now."

Chapter Five
River

I didn't sleep a wink last night.

Despite being physically exhausted in all the best of ways, my mind refused to shut off. Round and round it went, the focal point being piercing gray eyes that leave no room for argument.

How is this still a thing? Our contract has been burned, we need to make the marriage certificate disappear as well. Yet...

Just thinking about losing that last link to Marco gets my mind reeling all over again.

With a heaving sigh, I rise from my bed and grab my phone. I haven't even looked at my work phone for months. I didn't think I'd ever need to get back to that line of work since this huge contract landed on my lap—thanks, Tyler, for that thorn in my side—and turned my world upside down.

Maybe giving back Marco's money and opening a new account he knows nothing about wasn't my smartest move. In my defense, I don't like the idea of skipping out early on my contract and catching what I'm assuming are feelings for this guy. Taking money for a job, a clear contract, is one thing. Walking away because I got butt hurt—literally—is a whole different set of rules and I'm done breaking them.

Scrolling down my list of contacts, I pause on CAG as I pad my way to the kitchen. Thankfully, my downstairs neighbor loves to crank up the heat, but even so, nothing compares to how perfect the temperature was at Marco's home. Even with the marble floors. Here, I have to content myself with the worn-out carpet that seems to be standard in all the units of this building.

Oh well, gotta lose some to win some, I guess.

Although, I'm sure I could convince the landlord to allow me to renovate a little more than just the paint. He'd accepted that quite easily enough.

Setting up the coffee and digging inside my fridge for something substantial to eat, I sit at the kitchen counter and allow the aroma of the delicious java to awaken my brain cells. I've tried calling Nathaniel a few times without getting a single response from him. Each call went immediately to voicemail, and after leaving a couple of messages, I decided the ball was in his court.

Pouring a big cup, I add a little sugar and blow on the black gold, my mind trying to decipher what the hell is going on.

There are so many pieces of a very blurry puzzle that won't seem to come together.

Starting with Nathaniel and Marco's interaction at Mr. Bobby's funeral.

I rub my chest at the thought of my neighbor and friend who sacrificed his life for mine. All because Polly's bodyguard Frank was too much of a self-absorbed asshole to accept the word "no".

The men knew each other. That meeting was not a first, and judging from the animosity between them, they go way back.

And Tyler, too. At the gala, he said something about knowing Marco for a long time.

It can't be a coincidence that all three of these men in my life are somehow connected to each other.

Well, except for Nathaniel and Tyler. I've never seen them interact, but rich people run in rich circles so small they make mere mortals like myself dizzy.

Lost in thought, I jump when a message buzzes in my hand.

Husband: Did you sleep well, *Tesoro*?

It may seem like a simple question but there is no good answer to that.

If I say "yes", he'll assume it's that fucking orgasm that put me in a coma.

If I say "no", he'll assume it's because I've been thinking of him all night. And he wouldn't be wrong. *Fucker*.

Better to go with the third option. Deflect.

Me: I'm sorry, you have the wrong number. Please delete my contact.

Husband: Not happening.

Me: Then I'll have to block you.

Husband: Do it.

I scoff at his arrogance. Does he really think I wouldn't just block his number and be done with him?

Pressing on the little icon next to his name, my thumb hovers over the word "block". Before I can even make a decision, another message pops up on my screen.

Husband: Good girl.

I hate him.

And the muscle twitch on my lips isn't a smile, it's a scowl.

It's then an idea pops into my head and a devilish grin appears on my mouth. I suppose if he's keeping tabs on me, then I'll give him something to watch.

It's early afternoon on a Monday and the streets of Manhattan are vibrating with energy as my feet hit the sidewalk. Brand new week with brand new goals to meet. The ants are marching to their nine-to-fives, hoping for a promotion, prepping for a meeting, dreaming of a good old fashioned office fling. Women walk proudly with their shoulders back and chins high, men power through crowds like the entire world belongs beneath their knock-off leather shoes.

While ambition and power are the fuel to this city, the working class are the very heart of it. The small mom-and-pop shops, the food trucks, the men and women who clean our streets. *They* are the reason we thrive on tourism.

"Hey, Manny, what's up?" I wave at the thirty-something man who owns the barber shop down the street from me. This place is his pride and joy and keeping the sidewalk clean is something he learned from his dad, so no matter how many times he has to come out here and sweep the front, he does it with a smile.

"River! Where have you been, girl? Haven't seen you in a while." Yeah, the last time I came to this apartment was to save a marriage. I got a message from them a few weeks ago letting me know she was pregnant and I couldn't be happier for them.

"Been busy, but I'm back now!"

"Glad to see you. Don't be a stranger."

I opt out of taking the subway on the east end of Midtown since it's a complete waste of time, and by the time I reach the Medical Center, I feel like I've powerwalked the February chill right off.

As soon as I step through the office doors, I can tell something is off. Different from a few months ago.

"Hey, Shantelle, it's been a while. How are you?" Nate's secretary raises her head and gives me a bright, welcoming, smile.

"River! How are you?"

"I'm good, been busy. Is Nathaniel in?" At my words, her face morphs into confusion.

"Have you not been in touch with him lately?"

"No, why? What's going on?" Just as I finish my phrase, a burly man with a head of white hair and a clean-shaven face opens his office door and sees a patient out.

That is definitely not Nathaniel. My head snaps back to Shantelle and she just shrugs like she can't understand what's happening either.

"Showed up at work one morning and Dr. Reed was gone, and in his place was Dr. Lowell. Made sure my contract was honored and he didn't even take any of his patients with him. Strangest thing."

My face must mirror her confusion.

"I guess you didn't know either, huh?" Patting my hand like I'd imagine she does with patients who've just heard bad news, she tilts her head to her side and smiles kindly.

"I'm sorry, I can't tell you much more since I don't actually have any information."

I blink, trying and failing to make sense of all of this.

"Oh, yeah. Of course. I'll just... try his cell again. Thanks, Shantelle, I really appreciate it."

Outside, I step to the side to make sure I don't get in anyone's way and bite off one glove in order to use my phone.

On CAG's number, I press call and wait, my worry rising with every second that passes.

But just like the other times, the call goes straight to voicemail.

Did he block me? I'm not sure how that works and if I'd even notice it, but I've got one more place I can go.

Ten minutes later, I'm at his apartment, and where his name used to be on the mailbox downstairs, is a Shannon Finn, telling me he's moved out of this place, too.

Well, shit. Guess he doesn't want to be found then, does he?

Because I'm a glutton for punishment, I make a pit stop at my favorite grocery store. It'll give me the occasion to say hi to Francesca. I bet she'd be proud to know I've bettered my Italian comprehension skills.

I mean, I know what *dolcezza* means. And also *tesoro*. It's a start.

The little bell above the door rings out and I swear I jump at the sound as it transports me back to a simpler time. A time when I wasn't married to a mob boss and my Candy Aisle Guy was just a doctor buying wine in a mom-and-pop shop.

"River!" Francesca calls out my name, the "r" rolling like a tidal wave.

"Hi Francesca, how's it going?"

Coming out from behind the counter, she wraps me in a tight hug and kisses each of my cheeks.

"*Bella ragazza*! You are such a beautiful girl. But you lose weight, no? Too many bones, not good for health." I may have lost a couple of pounds, but I wouldn't say I'm all boney and shit.

"Well, I haven't had enough of your pasta." She beams at my words. Most of the food in her shop comes directly from Italy, the pasta being among those things.

The warmth at my back just as Francesca's gaze focuses behind and over my shoulder, is the only warning I get.

"Fancy meeting you here, Skittles." His hand is at my hip, his breath tickling my ear. It's a familiar touch, like homecoming after four years in college, I'd imagine. Like, it was home but now it's just a place to stay and visit.

Fucking Marco Mancini's voice runs in my head. *"Mine."*

Turning around, I put some distance between us by placing a hand on his chest. He smiles at me, his beautiful blues peeking through his dark eyelashes.

"Nathaniel! I've been looking all over for you." How weird that I'd find him here, where we first met all those months ago.

"My mother is not doing very well so I've moved back in with her." Immediately, I feel like shit for having doubts. He really is a good man, taking care of his ailing mother.

"I'm so sorry to hear that. I tried calling but…" I don't want to sound rude, yet here I am, being nosy.

"Yeah, lost my phone so I got a new one, but I don't have your number saved."

Makes sense, I guess.

"I left messages." Okay, that sounds accusatory, but fuck it, I did try to contact him and he completely ghosted me, so yeah, I need answers.

Nathaniel flashes his gorgeous smile at me and my brain cells backfire a bit.

"Did you miss me, Skittles?" His gaze falls to my hands, still pressed against his chest, and his grin widens. "Glad to see you've come to your senses."

It takes me a minute to understand what he's referring to, but when I see what he's staring at, I get it.

As though I've been burned, I pull my hands back and bury them both in my coat pockets.

"It's complicated."

"I bet it is. Marco's an onion, and at the end of the day, he'll make you cry." There it is, again. The familiarity between them.

"How do you know him?" I realize we're standing at the checkout counter of the store when a couple comes up behind Nathaniel and, with an annoyed look, lets us know we're blocking their access. "Do you have time to grab a coffee?"

"For you, I have all the time in the world."

Of course, we end up at the same coffee shop where we first had our date. Of course, he orders the same weird ass drink he did the first time. Strawberry something or other.

Unlike the first time, I'm distracted and a little hesitant. But this is Nathaniel Reed, I should be ecstatic that he's here. That I'm here. That we're finally together.

Except that fucking voice in my head is making me crazy. *"Mine."*

Pulling off my beanie, I shake my head to give my hair some semblance of control, and when I look back up at Nathaniel, he's got this wistful expression on his face.

"What?" My fingers in my hair, I try to tame the strands as best as I can.

"I miss you." It's the first time his words sound truly sincere. Like the honesty is pouring from every letter.

"Me too." That's when I'm reminded of all the questions I have and all the obstacles that kept us apart.

"How long have you been free from Marco?" Okay, that's it. I need to know what the fuck is going on.

The server brings us the drinks we ordered when we walked in, then promptly leaves us alone in our little corner of the coffee shop.

"Not long at all but, Nathaniel... how do you know him? This all feels like a weird coincidence and it's making me very uncomfortable." Wrapping my hands around the hot cup, I bask in the warmth it infuses in my entire body.

"I figured he would have told you but," he scoffs, shaking his head in disbelief. "I guess once a secret keeper, always a secret keeper." It sounds so ominous. But then, he's not any man, is he? He's a big deal in New York City with his luxury hotels and mob boss lifestyle.

"Well, can't say you're any better." I feel strangely defensive, like Marco's absence makes me his advocate.

"Touché."

"Go on, then." I settle into my seat and wait for him to talk.

"We grew up together in the Upper East Side. Went to the same prep schools and basically hung out with the same crowds. Practically known him my entire life." It all makes sense, I guess. Like I said, rich circles are incestuous.

Still, it feels stunted. Incomplete. It's hard to pinpoint what information is missing, but certainly there's more to it. Why the animosity at the funeral?

"The more interesting question is, how is it *you* know him?" Ah, this is the moment where I find myself at another crossroads.

To divulge or not to divulge? That is the dilemma.

Thinking back to Everest and his painful accusations, I decide in that half a second that it's time to come clean. If Nathaniel can't see past my job choice, then I was wrong about him on all counts.

"Well, it's not as simple as it is for you, that's for sure." Taking a sip of my coffee, I give myself a few seconds to gather my thoughts.

In the span of time it takes me to sip and swallow, all possible scenarios run through my mind.

He'll walk right out the door without a word.

He'll be shocked and accuse me of being a whore. A disease-ridden whore.

He'll be hurt that I've been lying to him for so long.

He'll be angry that I had clients while we were dating.

My hope holds out for the last one... He'll be understanding and hear me out.

"Nothing ever is, right?"

No, nothing is ever simple in my life, so here we go.

"Marco Mancini was my client." I'm hoping he'll catch on quickly so I don't have to give him the entire story.

"Client? What? Did you fall in love while you were working together?" Nothing in his voice gives him away. No anger, no surprise, no hurt.

"Not exactly. It all started with a message from Tyler Walker's secretary giving me a name and an address. I went, we met. We signed a contract, and the rest is history." As if the mere mention of Marco is going to make him magically appear, I scan the small shop to make sure he's not close.

I'm being paranoid. I'd know it if he were following me, right?

"A contract?" There's no venom in his question, only curiosity. In fact, I can't even find a hint of surprise, which makes no sense. It's not like being an escort is as common as selling real estate. Or maybe I'm not being clear.

"Yes. A contract." Taking another sip, I pull up my big girl panties and go for the gold. "I'm a high-end escort and Marco was my client." I brace myself for a similar reaction to Everest and Kai, expecting indignation and shock.

What I get is silence. Contemplation.

"This is the part where you tell me you're disappointed in my life choices." I'm using sarcasm as a weapon and a shield, because the pain from my brother's reaction yesterday still aches like a dagger to the heart.

"I mean, do I like the idea that you sleep with other men? Not even a little bit. But I'm in no position to judge your career choices, River." I want to feel comfort in his words, like he's accepting all of me. I want the relief of getting this information off my chest, yet there's a strange foreboding that's nagging me.

"Marco was supposed to be my ticket out." Nathaniel's jaw clenches at the mention of Marco, and his explanation that they were just classmates doesn't sit well with me.

"Supposed to be?"

"I gave the money back." With a shrug, I dart my eyes around the shop again, half expecting to see Marco.

"Shame. Bet he paid a pretty penny." Okay, so that felt uncalled for, but it probably has more to do with Marco than with me.

"Yeah, the offer was definitely appealing." *Not the man. Just the money.* I love the way my lie just invades my thoughts as though trying to persuade myself that Marco Mancini didn't get under my skin.

"So, it's over with Marco? He just let you go without a fight? Doesn't sound like him." *No shit.*

"Well, kind of. He's… stubborn. The divorce isn't final, yet." Nodding, Nathaniel smiles like he knows a secret before reaching out and taking my hand in his, kissing the knuckles and squeezing in reassurance.

"Have dinner with me."

"That sounds lovely."

As we leave the coffee shop, we agree to text a day and place, and when Nathaniel leans in to kiss me, I don't have time to back away. His lips land at the corner of my mouth, warm and inviting at first until I remember I'm still married. It doesn't matter that my marriage is only on paper, I'm not cheating on my husband. Not even a fake one.

And as Nathaniel backs away, a twinge of hurt shadowing his gaze, I hear that familiar voice with the slight accent echoing in my head.

"Mine."

Chapter Six

River

The half hour walk to Polly's club in Hell's Kitchen helps to clear my mind a little. The usual Sunday foot traffic, yellow cabs passing by at regular intervals, and the cool wind against my face all remind me that I'm alive and moving forward. There is nothing I can do about my past decisions and how I've handled them, there's nothing I can do about all the fucked-up shit leading up to the *super* fucked-up shit, so I just need to believe that the universe has a plan for me.

The police called a few days ago to update me on the case of a dick in a box, the shooting, and everything else, basically letting me know they don't have any leads yet. And as fucked up and twisted as it may seem, knowing that they'll never find anything put a smile on my face.

Nearing 10th Avenue, I pause for a moment. Polly's club, Rapture, is mere minutes away, and though I've stayed in touch with her secretary, Sheryl, over the last few months, this is my first time back since I married a mafia boss who helped me murder her head of security. We've touched on the subject of him being missing, she was worried to begin with, but after Sheryl confessed that he had not only abused her, but threatened her into silence, Polly seems to have dropped the search.

Thank fuck.

As much as the whole Frank thing still plays on my mind, I'm pretty sure it's not for the right reasons. I should feel awful about it, have flashbacks to the way the light left his eyes, but as with everything else about me lately, I'm broken. There's something inside me that feels satisfaction over what happened, and I won't allow myself to feel wrong about that.

Shaking away the thought, I take a deep breath and carry on toward the club. Today's when the new dancer is coming in for an interview, and I'm kind of excited about it. While Marco's payment would have set me up for life, after checking my finances, it seems I've actually got enough saved to buy this place anyway. It'll leave me with nothing, and everything I have will be riding on making a success of this, but I think I can do it. So this new dancer is hopefully the beginning of my new chapter. She'll be my first official hire—even though the place isn't officially mine yet.

The side entrance to the building takes me straight upstairs to the offices, where I'm greeted by a smiling Sheryl.

"Hey, Rose. It's so good to see you. You here to see Polly?"

"No? Is she back?" A grin creeps over my face at the realization Polly is back from her travels, though I'm also kind of sad that I have to hand over responsibility of the club again.

"Yeah, she's in her office. Head right on in." She shoos me away toward Polly's office, and I blow her a kiss before turning to walk through the door.

"Thanks, Sheryl."

"Darling! There you are. Don't you look delicious today? Come, sit." Polly gestures to the sofa by the wall as she gets up from behind the desk and joins me.

Running my hands over my royal blue wide-leg pant-suit, I turn to face her, a huge grin on my face as she grabs my face and air kisses my cheeks.

"How is that delectable husband of yours? Tell me everything."

My smile drops, my posture goes slack, and I look her in the eye with a shrug.

"Oh no, darling. I know that look. You broke the rules, didn't you?"

This woman can read me like a book—though it's not hard, plus she's the one who helped me hone my own people-reading skills.

"Yeah, kinda. But I broke it all off. I mean, we're still married, but not living together as a married couple anymore. The contract is now void, and I refused his money. That's about it in a teeny tiny nutshell." I shrug again, my go-to move when I'm uncomfortable talking about my feelings, which is most of the time.

"Well, there you go. And are you happy?"

What kind of question is that?

"Er, yeah?"

"Don't lie to me, darling girl. I'm far too old to be wasting time with lies." She raises a perfectly manicured brow, waiting for my answer.

"I will be. And that's what matters for now. Enough about my antics, I thought you were coming back next week. Is everything okay with you and your man?"

Polly smirks and subtly shakes her head with a roll of her eyes. I'm deflecting... I know it, she knows it, but she's going to go along with it anyway.

"Well, about that. Yes, everything is okay with me and Charles." My wide eyes as she began her sentence must have prompted her to reassure me before she carries on.

"I'm back early because I have a meeting with my lawyer. I was hoping you'd had enough time to think about my offer." Placing a hand on my knee, she smiles warmly at me. The crinkles by her eyes being the only things that give away her age.

Okay, so it's happening. This is a life changing moment for me, and I thought I'd be more prepared for it, but fuck it.

"Yes. I'd love to buy this place, Pol." Happy tears are prickling at my eyes, and I'm so fucking proud of myself in this moment.

I'm immediately engulfed in Polly and all her perfume as she wraps her arms around me.

"Excellent, darling. I'm proud of you, you know. Everything you've overcome, you're so resilient. Much like myself in my younger days. But please don't follow in my footsteps. Don't close yourself off to all opportunity when it comes to love. Being alone is wonderful, and I would recommend everyone try it out, but when you cross paths with that other half of your soul, then being alone will never be enough."

Pulling away, she bops my nose and stands up, moving over to her desk before turning to look at me.

"You've got a dancer to interview in ten minutes. You should get yourself ready for her and downstairs into the club. I'll have all the paperwork written up with my lawyer this afternoon." With a wink, she turns away and begins gathering things from her desk. I want to stay and help, but she's right. The new dancer should be here any minute, and I don't want to make a bad impression as her new boss by being late.

Her new boss.

Holy fucking shit.

Rapture is going to be mine.

I'm still trying to wrap my head around it as I make my way down the stairs from the mezzanine level of the club, where the offices area is sectioned off to one side, and the VIP area is off to the other.

Mimi, the newly promoted in-house security manager, waves me over to the bar as I reach the main floor.

"Has Lou-Lou arrived yet?"

"She's just getting changed out back. I told her I'd get the music queued up ready for when you got down here, boss." She winks at me, a knowing smirk on her lips. At first sight, Mimi isn't someone you'd place as security. She could easily pass as one of the dancers with all her curves—curves she keeps happily hidden underneath her self-imposed uniform; a loose-fitting, black, button-up shirt, black tie, black pants, and shit-kicker boots that make me green with envy. But after getting to know her over the last few years, she's not someone I'd want as an enemy. She's the kind of girl you want on your side in a brawl. I've seen her take down handsy men twice her size with a simple flick of her wrist.

"Not your boss yet, but I guess Polly's already spreading the news?" Making my way behind the bar, I grab a bottle of water, completely ignoring the fact that Polly's been telling people before it was even finalized. That woman's faith in me is mind-boggling.

"She mentioned something about you possibly permanently running things here. I'm happy for you, Rose. Want me to let Lou-Lou know you're ready?"

"Yeah, please do. I appreciate it."

"You got it, boss." She shoots a finger gun at me and walks away as I make my way over to a table in the middle of the room. It's the best position for the center stage.

Taking my seat, I put my water on the table and pull my personal phone out of my pocket. My work phone has been off and is currently sitting in a drawer in my bedside table. Having the club to deal with has been an easy distraction from taking on any new clients.

I pull up my messages, smiling at the last text I received from Nathaniel this morning.

CAG: Good luck with the interview today, Skittles. *wink emoji* *dancer emoji*

When he called me a couple nights after our coffee date for a chat, I'd told him a little about the club and the interview today. We haven't arranged a date for dinner yet, but I'm not in any hurry to organize that right now. I don't know whether it's because I'm still technically married and it feels all kinds of wrong to date other people, or whether my vagina is on strike, because I was dry as a whistle the last time we were together. Which never used to happen with Nathaniel.

The music begins to play before I have a chance to send a reply, so I close my phone down and watch the stage, ready for what I'm hoping is a good show. I'd hate for my first ever interviewee to be a dud.

Paint it, Black by Ciara fills the room, and I already like this girl. Her music choice is original and something on my own playlist. I can't wait to see what she does when the beat really kicks in.

The stage is all lit up, Lou-Lou has her back to me as she moves to the music. The way she moves is almost hypnotic as she twists and turns, throwing her lithe body around with ease. Her arabesque is over-exaggerated perfection, and I already know she'll fit in with the vibe of the club beautifully. My eyes widen as she turns to face me, and right there, dancing on the soon-to-be mine stage, is none other than Lina Mancini.

Is there no escape from this family? I mean, I love Lina, but really? Here?

She's too lost in the music to realize I'm the one watching her as she twirls and jumps and sways her hips with amazing skill. When she's finished, positioned on her knees, her back arched and an arm raised to the sky, she finally looks up. The stage lights are still hiding my identity, so I take a deep breath and steady my nerves for the conversation I'm about to have.

The fact that Marco has sent his sister in here to spy on me spikes my anger to unparalleled heights.

"Thank you, Lou-Lou. Can you exit the stage and come join me at the table, please?"

"Wait, I know that voice..." Lina stands, her eyes wide enough to match my own initial shock as she holds her head in her hands and moves toward me. "Oh my God, River! What are you doing here?"

"I could ask the same of you." I raise a brow at her and take a sip of my water. By the way the blood drains from her face, I'm thinking she's genuinely shocked to see me. Then again, maybe she's just a great actress.

"Please don't tell my brother about this." Narrowing my gaze, I scan her features, trying to find deceit on her part, but can't find any evidence of it. Her eyes—brimming with nervous tears—tell me she's actually scared of her brother knowing she's here. In a burlesque club. Dancing for the pleasure of others. Even with both of us seated at the table, she still won't look at me, repeating—no, begging—for me not to tell her brother. Finally, she peeks at me through her fingers and smiles shakily.

"Trust me, Lina, you don't need to worry about me saying anything to him about this. But I've got to say, I'm curious. Why are you here? I didn't think this was your kind of thing."

"You know I love to dance, and this is just so freeing, not like all the choreographed ballroom shit. The burlesque dancers in this place are renowned for their shows, and I want to be a part of that. I just need something new, fresh, and all mine. Not something easily handed over by my family with their stamp of approval. Although, with you here, I suppose I can't really say that anymore either, can I?"

Her answer makes me smile, I love her energy and drive to be who she wants to be. It takes a mere two seconds for me to decide how to handle this. I may be breaking another rule by having contact with an ex-client's family member, but this is Lina. The bundle of energy that wants to be set free. It has absolutely nothing to do with Marco. Nothing at all.

"Okay. That's good enough for me. Lina, your dancing is beautiful. You were mesmerizing to watch. But do you really think you can work here without anyone finding out?"

"Enzo's security team aren't as good as they think they are, although if he or Marco knew that, their asses would be fired. I'll just tell them I have more hours in the salon, and if it ever becomes a problem, I'll let you know. I'd never bring my drama to your door, River. But please, give me a chance? I need this." She's not quite begging, but I can see the pleading in her eyes that says she really wants this. It may be stupid of me to give in to her, but I'm a sucker for people following their heart. If this is what she wants, who am I to deny her the opportunity?

"When do you want to start?" I give her my biggest grin as I stand and open my arms wide for her.

She gets up from her seat and moves right into my embrace, whispering a heartfelt, "Thank you."

"You do realize Marco has the means to find out, right?" There's a sheepish look in her eyes as we pull away from each other, but her grin tells me a whole other story.

"Yeah, but I always manage to drop the security easily enough. They think I'm over at the salon today, so I've got a few more hours before I have to return to my diamond encrusted cage. Wanna grab lunch once I'm changed?"

"Absolutely. I'll meet you out here when you're ready."

I definitely shouldn't be going to lunch with Lina, but there's just something about the Mancini family that draws me to them when they're near.

Maybe I can get Petal to help me find a crystal or remedy to cure my growing obsession with making bad decisions.

Chapter Seven
Marco

"I'm telling you, man, she's up to something." I've got Enzo on speaker phone while I sift through the new remodeling plans I've been sent for approval. I've got a hundred different things happening at any given time, but Enzo believes my sister's whereabouts should be at the top of that list. It's not even close. On top of River's need to be independent and self-sacrificing, I've got that douchebag Eric making noise on the streets, talking about revenge. Stupid little prick. I regret not snuffing him out. Should have just ended him when I had the chance, but it was Christmas. Thought I'd spread the motherfucking cheer around.

"When has she not been up to something?" I don't know why this interior decorator thinks I'd be okay with baroque finishing all over my hotels, but right now, my priority is letting her know that Italian old-school is giving way to a more modern message. People truly believe Italy hasn't evolved since the days of Michelangelo if these designs are to be believed.

"This is different, Marco. I thought maybe she was sneaking off with Tyler Walker, but I put a tail on him." That gets my attention.

"Why the fuck would you put a tail on Tyler? It's no secret she's dating him." I've been so obsessed with keeping River safe and elevating my hotel chain to the next level that I have to admit, Lina's social calendar hasn't been on my radar.

"Don't fucking remind me." I don't know how he fucked it up with my sister. It wasn't hard to figure out that they were sleeping together. A blind man could see the way they looked at each other. He must have waited too long to let her in and she went grazing other pastures.

Unfortunately, she didn't go far and landed in the very green grass of my childhood best friend.

"So, instead of tailing Tyler, why aren't you following Lina? Isn't that your literal job description?" This shit is giving me a headache. Pressing the intercom button on my desk phone, I rub my temples as though that alone will stave off the pending pain.

"Yes, sir?"

"André, I need you to get"—flipping over the proposal, I search out the decorator's name—"Anita Schmitt on the phone, please."

"Right away, sir."

"*Grazie.*"

Throwing the godawful document in the trash, I focus on Enzo's need to control my sister's whereabouts. On the other end of the line, he's mumbling something about putting a tracker on her. Bad idea. And yes, I'm aware of my own hypocrisy.

"Lina knows how to find a tracker. We've taught her all the tricks since she was old enough to know about the family business. A tail is the best option."

"I can't put a tail on her because she knows every fucking way of losing them. She can recognize anything associated with the Mancini name from a mile away, which means she either disappears into thin air or, if she feels like having a little fun, makes them run around the entire city while she shops." I can't help the laughter that barrels out of my mouth and I know I'll get shit for that later, but it doesn't matter.

"Maybe, instead of obviously fucking up your chance to be by her side at all times, you should have let her in. Emotionally." Seems simple to me.

"Pot, meet the fucking kettle." He laughs, something Enzo does only on rare occasions and typically when he's had high-end liquor and enough alone time with Lina.

"The fuck's that supposed to mean?" Before he has a chance to answer, the intercom buzzes.

"Sir, Miss Schmitt is on line two."

"Thank you, André. Enzo, fix this yourself. I don't have time to babysit Lina. That's your job."

"By the way, River has a date with Nate tonight. Harlem Jazz Parlor, eight pm." That motherfucker hangs up before I have time to rip him a new one. He should have started our conversation with that instead of whining about Lina's apparent skills in losing her detail.

Poor Anita Schmitt takes the brunt—albeit reined in—of my frustration.

At ten past eight, I'm slipping into my seat, hidden in the back corner of the jazz room. As punishment, Enzo was summoned and forcibly asked to accompany me so I didn't look and feel like a complete psychopathic stalker.

I do not trust Nate. Not now, not ever.

Coming here was on a whim, a temporary loss of control, but the idea that River, my fucking wife, is on a date with that man had each one of my neurons misfiring. How else could I possibly explain the reason for braving end-of-day traffic in Manhattan as I made my way up to Harlem?

"This is hardly torture. Jazz is the best thing America ever created." I'm barely paying attention to Enzo's declaration for his love of jazz music because all the way to the front, I can see River's and Nate's backs and I'm doing everything I can to read their body language.

The simple, black, long-sleeved, skater-style dress she's wearing accentuates her beautiful curves, and all I want to do is bury myself between her thighs, wrapping her booted feet around my neck as she comes all over my tongue.

"America didn't create jazz music, slaves from Africa and the Caribbean did." I answer without moving my gaze from the woman who has consumed my every thought for months. I notice she's not leaning into his touch. Not looking at him the way I'd sometimes catch her looking at me. Not playing coy the way she used to.

Small mercies, I suppose.

"Same thing. It belongs to the American culture now, doesn't it?"

Fucker just put his arm around her shoulders like a preteen trying to make his move. From this distance, I can barely make out the heart-shaped birthmark on her neck as I contemplate a million and one different ways of ripping his arm off his shoulder.

"It's like spaghetti. Italians, we claim it, but it was born in China." Enzo's not going to like that.

"The fuck you talkin' about?" Predictable as always, his temper remains his weakest point.

"Marco Polo brought noodles to the west after he was introduced to them in China."

He scoffs. "You're an asshole. Noodles ain't spaghetti; two completely different things." I don't try to convince him that I'm speaking the truth because I'm barely keeping my control in check as Nate leans in and whispers something in River's ear. She's stiff, not giving him the signal that she's comfortable with his hands and breath on her.

"What can I get you to drink, sir?" The server startles me, my brain so focused on all the types of torture I could inflict on Nathaniel Reed I didn't even notice she'd stopped at our table.

"Whatever dark beer you have on tap." Enzo's arm blocks my line of sight as he reaches up and hands back the menu to our server.

"Make that two." Except I'm going to need something stronger if I'm supposed to keep my knuckles to myself. "And a top shelf scotch on the rocks." When I don't hear an answer from her, my gaze snaps upward, only to find this young, undoubtedly attractive woman looking down at me expectantly.

"Anything else, sir?" Her voice is suddenly sultry, inviting. Trying to pull me into her web of lust. But unlike my wife, I don't "date" other people. Instead of answering her, I lift my left hand and point to my wedding band with my right index finger.

Message received.

"Christ, your balls are tattooed on that ring, aren't they?" I don't think Enzo realizes he's playing with fire.

"Keep talking shit and your balls will be hanging from my rearview mirror." Just as I finish my threat, the jazz band gets on the small stage and begins tuning their instruments, one of the musicians giving us a small introduction that I don't bother listening to since the entirety of my attention is fixated on River.

I haven't once seen her give Nate any type of message that she's interested. I relax, just a little, knowing Nate is probably growing impatient that his plan is falling on its fucking face.

"He's not going to give up. You know that, right?" Enzo's rhetorical question is interrupted by the server, who sets our order on the table without a word and walks away.

"*Si*, it's why we're here."

"He's obsessed with her. That's a huge fucking *unpredictable* problem." He's not wrong

"She's mine and he needs to realize this." Without taking my eyes off River, I angle my glass so Enzo's can tap against it.

"*Salute*." In unison we literally wish good health to each other before taking a sip from our drinks.

I could polish it off in one gulp, but I'm not a savage. This is high quality liquid amber and I'm not wasting it, it deserves to be appreciated.

"Shoulda told her. I bet my way would have been more efficient."

"Your way has Lina running like a cheetah in the wild."

We both snicker because I've described my sister to perfection.

I freeze mid-chuckle as I watch River rise, excusing herself, before turning and walking away on the other side of the small parlor room. The lighting is dim, the tables filled to capacity, assuring me that she hasn't seen me.

"You're acting like a fucking creeper. Just go get your woman back and call it a night." Shooting him a raised brow, I say it all without speaking.

"Lina is not the same problem. She's... stubborn." Now, he's just making excuses.

"She knows what she wants and an emotionally stunted bodyguard isn't it." My words may seem harsh but he knows I'm right.

"Touché. Although—" I cut him off by rising from my chair and going after my wife.

The small hallway barely fits two people shoulder-to-shoulder, and lucky for me, it's empty. As I approach, I tell myself this is a terrible plan. River doesn't like it when I force her hand. Maybe Enzo's right, I should tell her what's going on, but I'm afraid her knowing would make things worse. Nate is content right now, happy to be winning.

Comfortable in his idea that he's on top of it all.

Me shaking the tree is only going to anger the wasp inside him.

The latch clicks and before she can fully open the bathroom door, I'm pushing her back inside, my foot slamming it shut.

"Marco! What are you doing here?" I'm guessing any other man would be begging for forgiveness, apologizing for being such an asshole, promising that I'll be better next time.

Except, I'm not that person.

"A little birdie told me my wife was out on a date." My hand flies to her delicate throat, fingers finding her pulse point. I revel in the spike of her heart rate, I can feel it through the throb of her artery just under the pad of my ring finger. On my left hand.

Fitting.

River stills, her lips parting and breaths coming in sharp and shallow.

"It's just a harmless date and you and me are not—"

"Do not finish that thought, River Mancini. In the eyes of the law and God, we are united 'till death rips us apart." Quickly, I lock the door before pushing her against the counter.

"Marco, you can't just—" My mouth slams against hers and suddenly, I'm home. Her taste awakens every cell in my body, amps up my adrenaline like no other. Her fingers find my shirt, pulling me into her as her luscious legs wrap around my waist, bringing us impossibly closer.

"I can, River. And I will."

My lips find hers once more and, with nimble digits, River unbuttons my shirt and slides her palms across my chest. She's warm and soft, heating my skin like lava to the side of a mountain.

"Show me your cunt, *Dolcezza*."

No hesitation, she spreads her legs and flips up her dress, revealing lacy panties with a fresh dark patch from her wetness.

"Is this for me?" I graze an index finger on the spot that cries my name.

"Yes."

"Take out my dick."

Her hands unfasten my belt and unzip my pants so quickly, I get a sense of satisfaction from her impatience. It mirrors mine, although I'm trying fucking hard not to show it.

My bet is that I'm failing miserably.

As my cock hits the cool air of the bathroom, I hear footsteps near the door, and instead of putting a stop to this insanity, I do exactly the opposite.

"Push your panties aside."

I love when she follows my orders, it makes me impossibly harder.

"*Bene, Tesoro*."

I'm inside her so quickly, I hear her gasp in surprise. We both exhale shakily at my sudden invasion, filling our lungs back up so I can pull out and fuck her senseless.

Any other man would slide his hand from her throat to her mouth to mute her screams of bliss. Except, I'm not any other man. I'm a man who revels in the pleasures of his wife. I'm the man who wants the whole fucking world to know she belongs to me. And only me. Nate fucking Reed can go fuck himself because one thing is sure, he won't be fucking my *dolcezza*.

With my other hand holding her in place at the thigh, I fuck her with determination. Our gazes locked, her pupils dilating with every rock of my hips, I brand her from the inside. With every thrust of my pelvis, I promise to be hers. I warn her that she's mine.

"Play with your clit, *Tesoro*, and give me your orgasm."

In a fraction of a second, her fingers are rubbing impatient circles around her hard, swollen nub. I pump in and out three times, a beautiful sound erupting from her open mouth and echoing around the powder room. Her pussy clenching my dick like a vice, squeezing my own climax from me and suddenly, I don't care about control. The only thing I want or need is to mark her.

To fill her with myself. To own her deep in her core.

"Goddammit, River. What have you done to me?"

We both freeze as I fill her to the brim. I'm coming hard and long, my orgasm like lightning in every nerve ending. Only once we're both finished trembling do I remove my hand from her throat and palm the back of her head, bringing her mouth to mine in a soul-scorching kiss.

We kiss for seconds, a lifetime, an eternity. It doesn't matter because my entire existence can be summed up in this moment.

When a fist bangs against the door, I pull out carefully, two fingers spreading my gift to her around her labia and clit before I pull off her panties, place them in the pocket of my pants, and give her one last longing kiss.

"When you sit back down with him, remember whose cum is inside your cunt."

Chapter Eight

River

After getting thoroughly fucked in the bathroom at the Harlem Jazz Parlor, it goes without saying that my mind was no longer on my date, which I'm sure was Marco's intention all along. Except now I feel like a cunt. Nathaniel has done nothing wrong. He's been kind to me, treated me with respect—even after finding out my secret—and he's given me a second chance after seeing me kiss my childhood best friend.

I should be swooning over this man, but I feel forever changed. I'm not the same person I was last year, when I was finding ways to get a peek at the sexy Candy Aisle Guy, living a double life and full of all the confidence in the world. Now, I'm married to a man I'm denying all attraction to, my secrets are out, and I'm a little broken inside.

Being broken isn't something I'm dwelling on though, it's an opportunity to grow and put myself back together so that I'm truly happy, not the fake happy I once pretended to be.

Buying Rapture is the first step toward my new future, and it gives me all the fluttery feelings inside to know I'm finally moving forward. After a phone call with Petal when I got home last Sunday, excitedly telling her all about it, she insisted I visit this weekend so Ev and I could talk everything out because his aura has been all off since the big reveal.

My impending visit to Staten Island tomorrow had me wanting to leave the jazz place early. At least that's what I told myself before we left.

The thirty-minute cab ride back to my apartment in Rose Hill is a relief. Knowing this date is almost over and I'll soon be climbing into my new bed fills me with a happiness I haven't felt all evening. Not even when Marco locked me in the bathroom with him, because that was just pure lust.

Pulling up outside my building, I step out of the cab, turn, and lean in to say goodbye to Nathaniel. Only, he's also getting out, and not headed straight home like I thought he would.

"Where does your mom live?" I'm curious, because his old place wasn't too far from me, but with him practically disappearing from around here, I imagined his mom lived quite a bit further away. Which means he should've kept hold of that cab to get home.

"I'd rather not talk about my mom right now, Skittles. If you know what I'm saying." He grins, that beautiful grin that used to make my knees weak. But all it does now is make me feel guilty for being full of another man's cum.

"Sorry, I have to get up early tomorrow to catch the ferry. No sleepovers for me tonight." It's a lame excuse, but it's all I can think of for right now.

Moving toward the building entrance, I take my keys out of my small black clutch bag before turning to face Nathaniel—expecting him to be where I left him on the sidewalk, and not halfway up the stairs behind me.

"A gentleman always walks a lady to the door." He smiles again, his eyes crinkling sweetly at the corners. Almost too sweetly as he leans in for a kiss. I know that's what he wants as his eyelids are at half-mast and his hand is reaching out for my waist.

Turning my head at the last minute, I give him my cheek, feigning a yawn so I don't come across as a complete bitch. It's not like kissing is something we've never done, he's not wrong for thinking that's where tonight could have led.

"Sorry, Nathaniel. I guess I'm just super tired this evening. Thank you for a lovely time though."

I unlock the entrance door, letting him know I'm ready to walk away.

"No problem, Skittles. I understand. Would you mind if I grabbed a glass of water before I leave?" Another step closer to me.

"Er, I don't know, Nathaniel. I think I need to be clear that nothing is going to happen with us tonight. I really am tired an—"

"Skittles, you don't need to explain. I genuinely would just love a glass of water before I head home." He's on the same step as me now, eagerly pushing through the door without me giving a response. His dominance doesn't give my vagina the same flutters it used to, and I'm kind of sad about that.

Shrugging my shoulders, I follow Nathaniel up the stairs to my apartment, pausing by my door to unlock it. As I do, I turn to him, a small smile on my lips.

"A glass of water, and then you go home. Yes?"

"Scout's honor." He strokes a cross with his finger over his heart and winks, causing me to laugh at his antics.

Opening the door and stepping inside, I'm immediately engulfed in a large pair of arms. I try to scream, to get away, but the hold on me is solid, and my mouth is covered with a hand almost as big as my face. That's when the smell of vanilla hits me, causing me to relax and roll my eyes at the caveman in my apartment. As I do, the hold on me loosens, and the hand at my mouth drops.

"You were never a boy scout, Nate."

Standing by myself once more, I put my hands on my hips and glare at Marco, who is looking all smug and pleased with himself as he smirks at me. He looks like a fucking model, standing there with his hands in his pockets where I know he's got my panties, the black shirt missing a few top buttons—which I think I'm responsible for—and showing off his tanned and toned chest that I had my hands on only hours earlier.

Marco's eyes travel behind me and his pupils darken in anger.

"Stay away from my fucking wife." His words are practically a snarl, and though I want to kick him in the balls for invading my space once again, his voice is hypnotic—in a has-a-direct-link-to-my-clit kind of way.

"I wouldn't say she was your wife. River has told me *everything*," Nathaniel snarks back. I feel my eyes widen at the venom in his tone, something I never thought him capable of.

With this macho stand-off happening in the entrance of my apartment, I roll my eyes again and step back so I can see them both argue about who has the biggest dick.

"Have *you* told *her* everything? Your intentions are no more pure than mine have been, Nate." The darkness that overcomes Marco as he speaks to Nathaniel should scare me, as should a lot of things about this man, but once again, I find myself feeling safe in his presence.

"I beg to differ." Nathaniel smirks at Marco before turning his attention on me. "I'll see you later, Skittles."

"Not if I can help it." Marco's words are said through gritted teeth to an empty doorway, as Nathaniel was quick to leave. His hands are now fisted at his sides, and his breathing is heavier than usual.

Shocked into some kind of weird silence, I'm still standing, staring open-mouthed at the interaction that just went on. The quiet lasts for a few short moments before I shake my head and address the fucking bully in my private space.

"What the actual fuck, Marco? What right do you thi—"

His lips are on mine—not for the first time tonight—and I'm cut off from finishing my rant. Angrily,

I pull away. I demand answers, and I won't allow his magical tongue to distract me from what I want.

"Marco, you can't just shut me up with your mouth every time I have questions. You owe me answers, and you fucking know it." My hands are on my hips again, and we're chest to chest, both breathing hard and fast. Well, I say chest to chest, I still have to look up at him to see his steel-gray orbs boring into me.

He closes his eyes for a second, taking a deep breath before answering me.

"On your knees, *Tesoro*. I'm going to fuck those dirty words from your delectable mouth." The angry snarls from earlier have turned into lustful growls, and I don't know why, but I obey the motherfucker. I can sense his control is on the verge of cracking, and I don't want to be responsible for that.

It has absolutely nothing to do with the way my nipples are pebbled against my bra and my pussy is soaked from not only his cum, but my own arousal.

Doing as he asks, I move to my knees and place my hands on my thighs—the perfect submissive position as I wait for him to present me with my treat.

His aura brightens just a little as he approaches, unzipping his pants and pulling out his beautifully hard cock.

Now standing in front of me, dick in my face, he grabs at my hair with one hand, tilts my head back, encouraging me to open up for him, just as he takes my panties out with his free hand. He brings them to his nose and inhales heavily, his eyes closed, like a fucking psychopath.

When did I become the girl who gets turned on by a mother fucking alpha caveman?

He slides in slowly at first, controlling my movements with his hand on my head. As he reaches the back of my throat, I relax my muscles and breathe through my nose—my eyes still water though, a natural reflex I've never been able to control when deep-throating.

"That's it, *Tesoro*. Take all of me."

I look up at him from the floor and his eyes are on mine, watching as he slides in and out of my mouth. I suck, hard, every time he pushes in, and run my tongue along the underside of his cock every time he pulls out. His movements get faster, harder as lust takes over his senses. The grunts coming from his throat spur me on to move faster, cupping his balls at the same time and rolling them around my hand. Releasing him with a pop and a final flick of my tongue, I take control—and he lets me, to some extent. I suck his balls into my mouth next, continuing to use my hand on his shaft as I do. His hand is on mine, controlling the speed of my movements as he groans again and again.

"Fuck this, I need to be inside you." He pulls me up by the shoulders, and I can tell by the way his face and body are tense that he was close to shooting his load.

His lips find mine once more, and he attacks my mouth with so much force I almost forget to breathe. His tongue battles with mine, and I revel in the way he worships my body with his hands all over me. They're traveling from my ass, to my hips, my waist, my breasts, my neck, it feels like he's everywhere all at once.

Grabbing my chin and tilting my head to the side, he bites at my neck before licking the painful mark and kissing down to my collar bone. He pulls the top of my dress down to reveal my breasts and immediately sucks a nipple into his mouth. Then, he moves his lips up toward mine, and before he can devour my mouth again, he spins me so my back is to his front. My couch is in front of us, and he pushes me to bend over the back of it, lifting up the skirt of my dress. There's a sharp slap of his palm against my ass, but the slight sting from his hand against my flesh is quickly forgotten as he slams inside me.

"Yes!" The word escapes my throat all on its own, and it's followed by Marco thrusting deeper, harder as he grunts his way to orgasm.

"Mine," is growled into my ear as he bends down, reaching around to grab my throat with one hand, his other finding my clit and torturing me to within an inch of my life.

The sensations my body is emitting are all full of fire and pleasure…

Marco knows exactly how to play my body to its fullest. I choose to ignore the *mine* comment, because this feels too fucking good to ruin it now.

"Come on my dick, *Tesoro*." Each word is punctuated with another thrust, and as his movements become erratic. I let myself go, allowing the building orgasm to break free all over this man. Tingles travel from my toes, up my legs, and as they hit my clit I feel my body twitching and clenching around his cock. Warmth fills me as he stills, and he rests his head between my shoulder blades, placing gentle kisses there which totally contradict his usual dominant demeanor.

After a few minutes, he pulls out, and I feel the best part of him dripping down my leg. Fun.

Before I can be bothered to move from my position—jelly legs make it difficult—I feel something warm move up to my thigh. Behind me, Marco is on his knees, a damp towel wiping away the remnants of him. He spends a little too long trying to shove his cum back inside me before cleaning that area, but I'm not complaining.

The moment feels tender in a way I have only seen from Marco a handful of times, but I can't allow myself to get used to this. He has to stop showing up whenever he feels like it. The sooner we get the divorce finalized, the better. I ignore the ache that thought provokes. Hell, it's probably just indigestion.

Now standing, Marco spanks my ass to let me know he's finished before he adjusts the top of my dress to cover me back up again.

"It's a shame to hide those beauties away, *Tesoro.*" He leans in to kiss my cheek before walking toward the bathroom to put the towel in my hamper. How he even knows where it is... is not a surprise to me anymore.

I don't respond to his comment, needing more information than I've had up to this point. Like why Marco still thinks we can be together without a contract, what the deal is with him and Nathaniel... and so much more.

I'll start easy.

When he's finished doing whatever the fuck he's doing in the bathroom, he joins me at the back of the couch, placing his hands on my hips, and encouraging my legs to open so he can stand between them. I comply, for now.

"Marco, I need to know what your relationship with Nathaniel is. You've both been talking in riddles, and I can't keep going on like this." I'm hoping my small amount of honesty here is received well, so I keep my tone snark-free for this very serious question.

The slow smile that forms on his lips warms his face, his eyes steady and soft as he places a kiss on my forehead. I'm sure he's about to leave my apartment without saying a fucking word, and I'm infuriated once again with this man. But before I have the chance to cuss him out for ignoring me as he opens the door, he turns to look at me, his features almost sad, and all he leaves me with is more confusion.

"In due time, my queen."

CHAPTER NINE
RIVER

"*I*n *due time, my queen.*"

Marco's words bounce around my brain for the entire ride across the Hudson. We both know he's keeping secrets, he's never pretended otherwise, but contrary to the secrets I kept from my family, his concern me directly.

It's like he and Nathaniel are playing with a mouse, bouncing it up and down and across the tile floor until they get bored and kill it. The only reason I'm not cutting them both out of my life is because I need to know what's going on and, honestly, I feel like Marco is completely invested in this. In us.

Sure, he's never denied wanting me, almost to the point of obsession, but this seems different.

Maybe that's why I keep falling into bed with him. Well, not *into bed*, per se, since I can't remember the last time we actually used one of those, but in any case, there's no denying my own all-consuming need for him.

My thoughts are interrupted by the sudden flurries falling like a white sheet, blanketing the steel ferry as it nears Staten Island. Dammit, this weather is going to do some serious damage to Everest's weekly earnings if he has to leave the market early. Still, I can't help the childhood memories this weather brings. Of times less complicated and filled with love and happiness.

"Mommy! Look! It's snowing!" The excitement boiling over from the little boy standing next to me is contagious. It is, in fact, snowing. I heard on the news that there was a chance we'd get the tail end of some Canadian snowstorm happening further north-west.

The advantage of not driving a car is that you can appreciate the small gifts from nature, snow being one of them.

Sliding my hands into my wool coat, I pull out my gloves and beret and get ready to face my brother. It's been two weeks since I've seen him. I've tried calling, sending texts, but I don't get much more than a one-word answer.

I get it, he's processing, but the hole his absence leaves in my chest is agonizing.

As the ferry gets closer to port, I ask an important question, trying to be honest with myself. Given the chance, would I do things differently a second time around? I don't have an answer to that, mostly because I can't see further than the need to provide for and take care of my brother. At barely eighteen years old with no high school diploma and the threat of seeing my brother being taken away by social services, I made the decision to do absolutely everything I could to keep what was left of this family together.

Lina: Hey SIL, if Marco asks, I'm with you.

Oh for fuck sake. Not only is Lina dancing at my burlesque club behind his back, but now she's using me as an alibi?

Me: This won't end well.

Lina: Pretty please with really expensive chocolate on top.

Me: I'm just saying, he'll kill us both.

Literally. Maybe not for her but it would be easy to get rid of my body.

Lina: LOL don't be a drama queen. He'll probably cut me off for like 48 hours.

Sure, and then he'll have Enzo kill me off like a bad character.

My stomach drops to my feet as the reality of my life starts to catch up with me with that thought.

Frank took so much from me; my privacy and my freedom. But mostly, he took my friend. And if I were inhabited by complete darkness, I would walk away from this guilt without a single glance backward.

But I'm not and I can't.

The floor of the ferry rattles and shakes as it docks in reverse into the port and every vibration travels through me. My breathing becomes shallow, my heartbeat a living, breathing monster in my ears. I can barely stand as I fight to keep breathing.

I'm holding a knife to a man's throat.

My hand shoots out to the wall of the ferry in an attempt to stay standing.

I slice the blade through his flesh.

People are crowding around me, talking, asking questions I can only hear through a faraway tunnel.

"Mommy, what's wrong with the lady?"

I can't breathe.

I can't stand and I can't breathe.

I can see the life fading from his eyes.

Screeching sounds echo all around me, people touching me, shouting words I can't comprehend.

I killed a man.

Oh, God, I can't breathe.

I killed a man.

I can't keep standing.

I killed a man.

Panic invades my every cell as the floor comes crashing toward my face, or maybe I go crashing toward it. I don't know.

I do not know.

I don't know anything except...

I killed a man.

After surviving the embarrassment of passing out on public transit and having no less than ten people ask me if they need to call paramedics, I slinked away, thanking the worried passengers profusely for helping me up.

The Uber ride over to Petal and Ev's house was blessedly quiet as I tried to understand what the fuck actually happened to me. It all seems like a blur; the dizziness, the rapid breaths, the idea that I was about to fall into some kind of black hole.

"Here, babe, have some water." Petal could see something was wrong the second she laid eyes on me. Bless her and that uncanny way she has of reading people.

"Thanks." With a slight tremble still visible in my hand, I take the offered glass and drink it all down like it might disappear in the next second.

"What happened?" Dammit. Barely two weeks since I laid out my entire secret world with promises of no more secrets, yet here I am, skirting the truth once again.

It's not like I can tell her, *"Oh by the way, I killed a man."*

"I think I had a panic attack. It's all just very blurry, can't remember all the details but, yeah…"

Petal sits next to me, one hand on mine as she rubs soothing circles on my inner wrist.

"Is it about you and my Bear? Because, Riv, he's miserable. I told him to call you but he can be so stubborn sometimes. And don't get me started on Kai. The amount of negative energy in this house is giving me a rash." Pushing up her sweater, she shows me the proof of her words. Right there, on both sides of her elbow, is a dark pink layer of skin with raised bumps.

"Does it itch?" Damn, that cannot be comfortable.

"A little, but I'm not worried. I'll take an oatmeal bath tonight and sleep with lavender on my bedside table." She pulls her sweater down and studies me like a puzzle she's trying desperately to solve. "I am, however, worried about you. You were so pale when you got here, it looked like you were about to pass out."

Okay, here we go.

"So, don't freak out but—"

"The fact you're telling me not to freak out is making my hives multiply, so just tell me." She's squeezing my hand, but as soon as she becomes aware of it, she adds, "Please."

"I did pass out on the ferry. But I'm fine. Like I said, it was a panic attack and all is well now."

It probably isn't, but I can't tell her that. I can't tell her that I've been walking around for months telling myself that everything is fine. Just fine. That I've been completely ignoring the traumatic event of... oh, I don't know... taking a life.

The fact it was Frank isn't the point. I can't find it anywhere in myself to regret him not walking the Earth anymore. Not just for what he did to me or Mr. Bobby, but for the pain and sexual assault he caused our girls over the course of all these years.

I just wish I hadn't been the one to actually hold the knife.

No, scratch that.

I promised I'd be honest, at least with myself. So, yeah, I'm glad I was the last person he saw when he died. Glad he knew I was the one taking his life.

And that, right there, is the reason I'm losing my shit.

This lack of remorse because it was Frank is making me question my entire existence.

But I can't tell Petal this, so I go with the least surprising alternative.

"I think this distance with Everest is not helping."

Fuck, good job, River. Blame your homicidal acts on your fucking innocent brother.

"Aw, Riv. It'll all work out. I promise. He's not okay with this distance either and I swear, he and Kai are just being stupid boys." We both chuckle but there's no real humor in it.

"I have to tell you something." With her head bent and eyes trained solely on her worrying hands, she's the one freaking me out this time.

"Okay, so now *I'm* worried. Please don't tell me someone's sick or died. I don't think I can handle that today." Throwing myself against the couch, I slouch like a teenager who's just been told she can't go out with her friends.

"No, Gorgeous, nothing like that, but I just… I think it's best you hear it from me." Her voice is barely audible with a hint of sadness. I don't like it.

"Okay, I'm ready. Just rip off the bandaid and let's see if it bleeds." God, I hope it doesn't bleed. I've had enough of that too.

"I think Kai and Freya set a date for the wedding a while back. I overheard them whispering about something happening right after your birthdays."

It takes me a few seconds to register what she's talking about, but when I do, there's that familiar pang in my stomach. Except, it isn't all-consuming. It doesn't take my breath away. I'm sad because I honestly don't think they're made for each other, and a date so close to our birthdays feels like they're encroaching on our special time, but I'm not heartbroken like I expected to be.

"Wow, that's in like, what? Three weeks? I mean, it's about time and all, but a little heads up would've been nice." It's my turn to grab Petal's hand and reassure her that I'm okay. In a long list of fucked up shit in my life, this isn't even on my radar.

"I guess you're right. Also, I don't think she's pregnant. Seems like she'd be ready to pop by now, you know?" Oh yeah, that was our theory for the quick announcement, but between the long engagement and the lack of baby bump, I'm with Petal. That said, I still think they're hiding something. Hell, Kai hinted at it at my wedding. Something about me not knowing the whole story.

"We'll find out soon enough, I guess." Bumping my knee to hers, we giggle, and again, it feels off, but I guess it's to be expected.

With a huge hug, she squeezes me tightly to her and just as she releases me, the guys both come barreling through the back door.

"It's snowing pretty damn hard out there, Pet. Did you see th—" As soon as Ev's gaze falls on me, he closes his mouth and comes to an abrupt halt in the living room.

Kai walks right into him, his phone falling to the floor making a thumping sound on the wooden planks. "What the fuck, dude?"

"Hey." I sound shy, like I barely know them anymore. Then again, maybe that's how they feel about me too.

"Sup," they both say in unison, and I recognize that tone. It's the way they both talk when they're trying to keep someone at a distance.

"Were you able to sell anything in this weather?" Petal saves the day by asking important questions.

"Some, but we had to put the rest in storage for tomorrow." With a nod, Ev runs upstairs and the room falls a couple degrees colder.

"What's going on? Why are you here?" Jesus, I can't visit for no other reason than to see them now?

"Nothing, I just wanted to spend some time with you all." Kai looks to Petal as though to verify my words, and that just pisses me off.

"What's your problem, Kai? I mean, do I suddenly need your permission to come visit my family?" He doesn't respond, just stands there staring at me like he doesn't know who I am anymore.

"Are you seriously not saying anything? I mean, you've always got a fucking opinion, so go on. Say it." My heartbeat is accelerating all over again so, to avoid another panic attack, I take in a deep breath and try to exhale slowly. Petal places a hand on my back, rubbing circles again like she always does to make us feel more grounded.

"I didn't say anything, River. I'm just surprised, that's all."

"Surprised that I'd be here?" I'm standing now, circling the couch to get in his face.

"To be honest, yeah. He's not ready for you to be around. Do you even know how much you hurt him?"

Of course I know. I feel guilty enough as it is, I don't need Kai throwing it back in my face.

"He's been feeling guilty these past two weeks because here he was, living his happy-fucking-go-lucky life, while his only living relative was putting herself in danger every fucking day." Little by little his voice rises until we're in each other's faces, our chests heaving like we've just run the New York marathon.

"Kai, that's enough. I don't need you fighting my battles." Everest is in the middle of the stairs, wearing different clothes and with his hair pulled back. It's been getting longer, just like his scruff is turning into a beard. As he comes to the bottom of the steps, I notice he's still limping a little, but his boot is off.

"Right on. Sorry." He answers Ev, but he's looking straight at me.

"Okay, I'm tired of this oppressing energy." Petal walks to the cupboard she keeps by the chimney and opens the bottom drawer, taking out an ornate wooden box. "Bear, you need to take this and go outside on the porch with Riv. Smoke it out, talk it out. I don't care. But this ends now."

We all look at her, our mouths dropped open, as she hands the box to her husband and then looks at Kai.

"You…" She points an accusing finger at him. "Stay with me. We need to put the rest of the veggies in storage."

No one argues with Petal. How could we? She always has our best interests at heart. I can count on the fingers of one hand the number of times Petal has raised her voice, and every time it's been for our own good.

So, that's what we do.

My brother and I get comfortable on the porch as he lights a joint, takes a hit, then passes it over to me.

"Petal and I have talked about this for a while. We tried to get to the bottom of my feelings and why I'm so angry with you." Leaning forward, he rests his elbows on his knees as he stares off into the back yard.

"I get it, Ev. I betrayed you."

"It's not that." I hand him the joint back and watch as he burns the paper and weed with a hearty toke. "You're my sister, Riv. I mean, I've got Petal—thank fuck—and Kai, but at the end of the day, you're my only blood relative. It's always been you and me and I really thought we trusted each other enough for you to tell me everything. Plus,"—he hands me back the joint and blows his smoke into the night air—"you basically put the blame on me. I felt like shit for weeks."

"Fuck, Ev. I'm so sorry, I really am, and I do trust you, I promise. But it's not something you can announce at Sunday brunch, you know?" It's my turn to take another hit, and I swear it eases my stress like nothing else.

"We don't do Sunday brunch." *Smartass.*

"You know what I mean."

"Yeah." Silence falls for a couple minutes before he speaks again. "I love you, Sis, but I'm not ten anymore. You can't make unilateral decisions to keep shit from me to supposedly protect me." He faces me then, his eyes still carrying the burden of my lies. "We should be protecting each other, Riv, but I can't do that if I don't know what's going on."

I have a moment of guilt knowing I cannot and will not admit to murder, especially if it also implicates Marco. It's not the same though. No one will ever know about Frank so that's a moot point.

"You're right. When I told you guys everything a couple weeks ago, it was awkward on my part. I didn't mean to blame you for anything, seriously. Back then, I was trying to prove something to myself, maybe to prove that I could keep our family together. More than anything, I wanted to keep Daddy's promise alive. I could have done a million other jobs but I chose this path. Me, alone. I guess I was enjoying playing dress up and living the life of someone else." Looking up at my brother I can see he's beginning to maybe understand and that relieves me of some of the guilt. I hold out my pinky and he does the same. "No more secrets?"

"Pinky swear to stay truthful." Fuck, I'm going to Hell with a VIP card around my neck and Marco in the driver's seat.

Some of the strain between us dissipates, but there's one thing I need more than anything.

"Ev?"

"Yeah?" He finishes off the joint and turns to me.

"Can I get a bear hug?" The grin that spreads across his handsome face gives me life.

"Get over here, you goofball."

It's then that Kai and Petal join us, two more joints in hand. For the first time in I can't remember how long, it's just the four of us. It's familiar and comfortable even though it isn't perfect yet since Kai is still a little distant, it's close enough to ease my mind.

Finally, something is going right in my life.

Chapter Ten

River

A few days with Ev and Petal has helped to put a new spring in my step. I hadn't realized how much I really needed to talk with my brother, and now that I have, it's like a small weight has been lifted. When everything else is going wrong, I have always been able to go to him to find some semblance of peace and belonging, and I almost fucked all that up.

I'll never be the same person I used to be, but things are starting to look up again, and I can start to work toward the new, revised version of myself. The pain of everything will always be there, I just need to learn how to live with it.

My work phone has officially been off since before Christmas, meaning I have had no new clients for a long-ass time. But as I make my way to Rapture to meet Polly, I can't help but wonder how some of my ex-clients are doing. My one yearly client might not even be aware

I'm basically out of the business these days, maybe I could put him in touch with one of Polly's girls. It'd have to be one willing to engage in watersports, but I'm sure someone would take the job.

Okay, I'm here. Deep breath, River. Today is the beginning of the rest of your life.

Looking up at the large, glowing red sign for Rapture, I smile. When I walk out of this building after my meeting with Polly, this place will officially be mine. A thrill races up my spine at the thought. It's taken Polly mere days to organize her lawyers and the contracts, and I didn't realize how quickly things could move in this situation. I was expecting it to be months before I was finally able to take over, but it's a week and half before my birthday. So I decided this is my twenty-seventh birthday present to myself.

I spent hours discussing my plans for the burlesque club with Ev and Petal while I stayed with them, and they're almost as excited as I am by my new venture. I dressed for success today, in black wide-leg pants, a red silk button-down shirt and my favorite black Jimmy Choos, and I feel like a fucking goddess as I enter the office space upstairs.

"Hey Sheryl. Polly in her office?" I know she is, because she's never late to a meeting, but it's polite to check.

A huge smile creeps onto her face when she looks up at me, and she practically throws herself out of her chair to give me a hug. "Yes, she is in her office, but I hear it won't be hers for much longer. I'm so excited for you, Rose! Go on in." She shoos me away as she heads back to her desk, using the intercom to buzz through to Polly at the same time as I open the intricate black door.

The details of this place are catching my eye more than usual on this visit, and I think it's because it's almost mine. I want to squeal like a school girl who hasn't seen her friends for a few days, but I rein it in. With a deep breath, I enter the room. Polly is sitting behind her large desk, and I'm assuming the lady opposite her is the lawyer she was telling me about, here to notarize the documents as we sign them.

"River, darling, you look stunning." Polly rises from her chair and walks around her desk to air kiss both of my cheeks.

"Thanks, Polly. As do you." And I'm not just saying that to be kind. The way her beautiful green dress clings to her curves makes you forget her age.

"Okay, let's get to it then, shall we? I see no reason for us to discuss anything further than we already have." Sitting back in her tall black-leather chair, Polly pulls the paperwork over to herself and signs on all the dotted lines before pushing it in my direction.

"Are you sure you want to do this, Polly?" I know it was all her idea, but I'm essentially buying two businesses and she's not charging me anywhere near as much as she should be.

"Oh shh, darling. Of course. We've been over this a hundred times. I'm perfectly happy, and you need to do this. Plus, I'm looking forward to spending some more time with you while you get settled into it." She raises a brow at me and stands, gesturing for me to sit in her chair.

This feels like a monumental moment. No one ever sits in Polly's chair if she's in this room, it's like an unspoken rule. She smiles at me and hands me the pen as I pass her, then she kisses my forehead and pushes me down by the shoulders to sit.

Deep inhale.

I can do this.

On an exhale, I position the papers in front of me, finding the first dotted line, and hover the tip of the pen just above it.

"Go on, Darling."

With every scratch of the pen over the documents I've read nearly a hundred times since Polly emailed the final draft to me, I finally feel more in control. More like myself again.

There.

It's done.

I own a fucking burlesque nightclub and a private escort service—I may have told my family the whole truth and come clean, but I never said I was out of this world forever.

As if my body has a mind of its own, I jump from the seat and turn to squeeze Polly, almost knocking the bottle of whiskey out of her hand.

"Where did that come from?" Her hands were empty before now, so I'm curious to know where all the hidden drawers and things in this room are, because I know they're here. Polly is renowned for secret cubby-holes.

Tapping the bottom of the desk twice, she grins as a small wooden flap opens, revealing a bottle-sized hole. Then she winks and hands me the bottle.

"A celebration present, Darling. I know you prefer this stuff over champagne. How does it feel to own multiple businesses?"

"Honestly, it feels fucking amazing, Polly. Thank you so much for everything you've done for me." I stand and we hug again, spending the next couple of hours discussing the ins and outs of the businesses. The escort side of things and the nightclub side of things are both pretty much at a point where they run themselves with all the staff Polly has in place, but I will be making some time to introduce myself to everyone properly soon.

First things first, though. It may only be four in the afternoon, but I need to celebrate.

Mimi is by the entrance as I'm leaving, a wide smile on her face when she sees me approaching.

"Afternoon, boss."

"Hey, Mimi." Her grin is infectious, and I can feel my own growing by the second.

"You know where I am if you need anything, Rose." She winks and opens the door for me.

"About that... you can call me River." I don't explain, I just return her wink and walk out of the building, that spring in my step even bouncier now.

Fuck, that felt good.

I'm officially a business owner... a legal business owner—because the tax man doesn't need to know where the additional revenue stream comes from. Everything I've done up to this point has been executed with secrecy, worry, lies. Now, I'm becoming the me I've always wanted to be.

I've made up with my family—even though Kai is still being douchey with me—and I'm now an official business woman with my own club. There are still a lot of fucked up things surrounding my life right now, but that's all fall-out from something I'm trying to leave behind, so I guess two out of three ain't bad.

Taking out my phone, my automatic reaction is to call Marco and tell him my good news and ask him to join me, but I hesitate. Why would I call Marco? Shaking my head, I scroll through my contacts and pause over Nathaniel's nickname. *CAG*. Before I can press call, Lina comes barreling out of the entrance to the club.

"River! Oh my God, you're my new boss? That's epic. Come on, we're going to celebrate. No, wait, stand in front of the building, let me take a picture."

She's a whirlwind of words, as usual, but I laugh and do as she asks, posing for a picture or ten in front of my new building.

We've been dancing for the last two hours after bar-hopping across most of Hell's Kitchen, and though I'm not really dressed for it, I don't give a shit. I'm not here for any other reason than to celebrate a new chapter in my life with my soon-to-be ex-sister-in-law. Lina, on the other hand, is perfectly dressed for the dance floor. In her jean hot-pants and yellow halter-neck top, she twists and moves her body to the beat, catching the eye of several guys surrounding us.

I get the impression she's not interested though. From what she's told me, her heart is currently torn in more than one direction. Adding a few more to the mix would only further complicate things.

The combination of lights, music, and alcohol flowing through my system do their job in helping me let go and enjoy myself.

"Oh my God. Yaaaas!"

Lina's excitement matches my own as the anthem of all anthems begins to play, and the dance floor goes wild at the first few bars of iconic music.

"I fucking love this song!"

The sweat dripping down my spine is quickly forgotten as Lina and I jump around, singing every single lyric of *Girls Just Want To Have Fun*. This is the most fun I've had for a really long time and I never want this day to end. I wave my arms around my head, swaying from side to side with a smile so big my cheeks ache.

As the song comes to an end, I'm ready to carry on to the next one, but Lina is looking a little worse for wear. She did tell me she's a massive lightweight, but insisted on matching me shot for shot.

"Come on, you. Time for a glass of water, then I think we should get a cab home."

A gleam of excitement fills her gray eyes—so like her brother's. "You're coming back with me?"

I sigh, a pang of sadness shooting through my body at the thought. "No, babe. I'll share a cab with you, drop you off, then head to my own home. Sorry." And I really am sorry. For so many reasons.

"Oh. Okay."

It doesn't take long to reach the bar, and I ask the bartender for two bottles of water with Lina by my side. A dark-haired guy with a Superman-esque body hovering by the exit catches my eye, but before I can get a good look, he's gone. For a moment, I thought it could have been Nathaniel, but I don't imagine this kind of place is his scene.

"Can we buy you ladies a drink?"

Oh no. These are the dudes who have been eyeing Lina up all night. From the greasy hair to the glassy pupils, I'm guessing these guys have been playing with more than just recreational drugs. One guy tries to speak to us but I can't understand a single word he's trying to say, his slurring is so thick. The other is trailing his gaze up and down our bodies like he has x-ray vision. I suddenly feel dirty and the only thing I want to do is get the hell out of here. Or, kick them in the fucking balls. And if they make a move, I will definitely do the latter.

"No, thank you. We're about to head home." I give a tight smile, not wanting to encourage them.

"Well, you're about as fun as a paper bag. What about your exotic friend over here? I bet you'd like a drink, wouldn't ya, sexy?" The shorter of the two men gets far too close to Lina, stroking his hand down her back and squeezing her ass as she leans over the bar next to me, completely ignoring them.

She doesn't react immediately, instead she slowly turns her head to look at the creep, and I'm ready to step in, but I know how important it is to handle your own shit in these situations. I don't want to take away her moment to defend herself, even though I'm watching every movement carefully. Just in case. She is drunk, after all.

"If you don't get your hand off my ass, you're going to lose it." The usual cheery smile on her face is gone, replaced with a darkness I've only ever seen in her brother.

The blonde guy steps forward, putting his arm around my shoulder and I don't think. I push my elbow back, hard, into his stomach, hearing a grunt and a, "You fucking bitch."

Spinning away from Lina, the short guy leers at me, anger clear in his mud-brown eyes. Before he can move any closer, I sharply lift my knee, knowing I've hit my target as soon as the little dick crouches over in pain.

Lina's smile becomes genuine once more, and she winks at me before holding her hand out for me to take. "I think I need to puke. Ladies room then cab?"

"Sounds like a plan."

After listening to Lina's insides reaching the bottom of the toilet bowl as I held her hair back, we're now both washing our hands.

"You remind me of Tyler's sister, you know. She used to hang out all the time when she was with Nate. I remember this one night we went out, and she ended up kneeing some jerk-off in the balls for attempting to touch her. Fucking epic. I still miss her."

Wait, *what?*

Just as I open the bathroom door, my other hand pulling Lina behind me so I can take her home, excruciating pain on my cheek stuns me, my head slamming into the door jamb with the force of the hit.

Despite the surprise and the red-hot sting to both sides of my face, I have the wherewithal to protect Lina. I barely get my bearings enough to see the guy who hit me is the same one I kneed in the balls fifteen minutes ago, before all hell breaks loose in the hallway.

"Come with me!" Enzo is standing in front of me, his gaze traveling over Lina like a body scan, probably assessing her injuries, if any, before deciding if someone is going to—literally—die tonight.

So, if Enzo is here, who is on the floor beating the shit out of the guy from the bar?

My watery eyes—a side-effect from the throbbing on my cheek—dart to the men on the floor. One is pummeling the other, blow after blow, his arm a legit weapon, when Enzo pulls him by the neck and ushers us all outside.

The inner feminist in me wants to rip them both a new one for rushing in and being the saviors no one asked them to be. But the reality of the matter is that I've never been happier to see Marco Mancini—in all his murderous glory—standing in front of me.

Chapter Eleven

Marco

I t's rare, but like anyone from her generation, announcing achievements on social media is par for the course. This is how we knew that Lina was with River celebrating the leap into her new business venture. Coupled with my own sources, I learned that they were drinking and dancing at the nearest club, and apparently tequila was on the menu.

That last bit of information is the reason Enzo and I are sitting in the dark corner of the club, keeping an eye on our girls. Needless to say, I didn't have to ask him twice to join me.

Where River's club is classy and held to an impeccable standard when it comes to respect, The Sandbox is the complete opposite. The men in here are fucking predators and the only reason women keep coming is because the DJ has a world-renowned reputation and delivers every time.

We won't intervene unless absolutely necessary, but I can't just sit home and wonder if River is okay. I need to make sure. I have to be certain that my wife is safe at all times. Not to mention my sister, who only sees the good in people.

Well, until she doesn't.

When the fucking douchebag puts a hand to her ass, I have to physically hold Enzo back by the shoulder or risk having to hide another body in the East River.

When the douche's friend cages River in, it's Enzo's turn to hold me back.

We both relax as our women hold their own. I swear Lina's face is feral. Her eyes, so much like mine, turn to knife blades as she snarls something I can't hear to the first guy. But my night is completely made when River knees the other guy in the balls.

"*Salute,*" we both say, proud grins on our faces, as we tap the whiskey glasses together.

"So, tell me something. How's this whole thing with you and Tyler work? Is she dating both of you until she chooses who she wants?" I'm genuinely intrigued here. I've known these guys for a long time—Tyler practically my entire life—and never would have pegged them for sharing anything let alone the women in their lives.

"No one's asking her to choose."

What? Enzo is a bit of a lone wolf, his trust is limited to those he'd die for and Lina is definitely in that category. Tyler? I didn't think so, but apparently, I was wrong.

"Okay, then. So, what? You've got a calendar or something?" Then a thought occurs that makes my hot, Italian blood suddenly heat to dangerously temperatures. "Are you fucking time-sharing my sister like a Goddamn condo in Miami?"

"Shut the fuck up, Marco. This is Lina's business. If she wants to talk to you about it, she will. We're done here."

I don't know what the fuck is going on, but I need to have a serious conversation with my sister to make sure she's okay.

Which reminds me...

"Where are they?" My spine is ramrod straight, my eyes scanning the entire dance floor in seconds, trying to locate River's red button-down shirt to no avail.

"Fuck. I can't see them anywhere." Our gazes meet and just like so many times before in our lives, we make a decision without a single word.

With panic rushing through my veins, in unison, we rise from the sheltered booth and head straight to the bathroom area, the only place that would make sense. We haven't seen them in ten, maybe fifteen minutes. I'd feel much better knowing they've actually left, but something inside me, call it a sixth sense, tells me they're here.

Just as we reach the long hallway, I catch a glimpse of the moment the back of the greaser's hand connects with my wife's cheek, the other side of her head bouncing off the wooden frame of the door.

I. See. Red.

A veil of white-hot rage fills my tunnel vision, my entire body primed for the kill as River's cheek blossoms into a fiery red splotch. Enzo knows me, knows that right now, I have murder in my veins and a lion's view of my next kill. He goes straight to River and Lina while I tackle my wife's attacker.

I don't think, I don't fucking care that we're in a public place where anyone, from cops to serial killers, can witness the beat down I'm giving this piece of shit. The knuckles of my right hand plow into the same spot, over and over again, as I break his nose into a thousand shards of bone and cartilage, while my other hand is holding him down by the throat. Blood is everywhere. All over his face as he gurgles in it. No doubt all over my suit and shirt and probably my face.

"You think you can touch my wife?" I hit him again, the crunch more of a squish now. "You think I'll let you live after you dared hit my wife?" I can't imagine he can hear my words, he's close to passing out or, Hell, dying from the force of my fists against his face.

I don't give a fuck.

He backhanded my wife. He doesn't get to live to tell about it.

I'm about to deliver my final blow, the one I'm convinced will send him to another realm, when I'm pulled back by my collar, another arm under my shoulder.

"You piece of shit! I will find you and I will kill you." I'm aware that I've completely lost my mind. Control, usually my constant companion, has abandoned me and left me with utter chaos.

He hurt your wife.

The thought bounces around my brain and I'm ready to end him all over again.

But Enzo is there, trying to get through the curtain of red rage that's blinding me to anything but the kill.

"Marco. Oh my God, are you okay?" It's her voice that gets my attention; that has the crimson vision receding to a more respectable place in my mind. It echoes from one end to the other until I turn toward the sound. When my eyes land on the angry streak of red still blazing on her cheek, I wonder if I could murder the same person twice.

I don't answer, just stalk toward her and place both of my hands on the sides of her face and slam my lips to hers. I need to feel her heat, to know she's okay. I need her to make me see clearly again.

We kiss like the fate of the universe depends on every lick and bite we share.

"Let's go." Enzo is walking away with Lina, his phone to his ear, and I'm guessing he's calling the clean-up crew. Two women pass us in the hallway and seconds later scream at the top of their lungs. River stands in front of me, and just when I'm about to pull her to the side, she looks over her shoulder and shoots me with a murderous glare of her own.

That's when it hits me.

She's protecting me. Masking the blood on my shirt by walking just in front of me.

My wife cares. I smile at the thought, my entire body humming with the knowledge that I've gained a little bit of ground with her, even knowing damn well that when we get home—and yes, she's coming home with me god-dammit—she's probably going to rip me a new one.

I'm looking forward to it.

The car ride back to Fifth is quiet on my end. I don't speak, my eyes never leaving the red spot on River's cheek, while Lina is talking a mile a minute about how she wants to go back and beat the shit out of the guy herself. About how River was protecting her. About how bloodied up I look even though Enzo reassured her that I'm fine. The guy didn't even get one punch in. How could he?

I'm a man who loves control, lives and breathes it on a continuous loop. But when it comes to River Fox-Mancini, it all evaporates like a puddle on a New York summer's day. There one second, gone the next. I've realized in the last few weeks that she is her own person as well as mine. She may be a Mancini by marriage, but she is still a Fox, and I don't want to be responsible for stripping everything she is away from her. Who knew I could evolve at the ripe old age of thirty-two?

River's eyes never leave mine, her chest heaving, the adrenaline probably racing through her bloodstream just like it is for me. There's worry and fear and just enough of a hint of lust to give me hope for later.

By the time we've reached the house, Lina is passed out in Enzo's arms and River is hesitating on her next move. She may think I don't know her, but I do. Those little things that people deem inconsequential, the things I've trained myself to take notice of, are the things that build the very core of our character.

The way she always focuses on other people when she doesn't want to make a decision about herself.

The way she straightens her spine and squares her shoulders when she readies for a fight.

The way her face goes straight into resting bitch mode when her walls go up like a steel curtain of protection.

The way her nose wrinkles when she laughs with abandon.

The way she comes on my tongue with her fingers buried in my hair, pulling to the point of pain.

I know her.

And I know, right now, she's thinking about bolting. And because I've been studying her, I know how to make her stay.

"She's going to need you in the morning, *Tesoro.*" Because I'm a fucking asshole appealing to her need to care about others, but *she* already knows that.

"That's a dick move, Mancini, and the only reason I'm going along with it is because I think she actually *will* need me in the morning." Stepping close to me, her body flush against mine making every cell boil with anticipation, she leans in and almost—fucking almost—brushes her lips to mine. "Since the two of you can't keep your fucking tempers in check."

River steps away after delivering her blow, but I catch her around the waist and pull her back where she belongs. "That's two, *Tesoro*. Better believe I'm keeping count."

Our mouths crash together, all tongues and teeth and moans. We kiss until I can't feel, or even think about, anything but the taste of her. We kiss until I realize I've never been in anything more real in my entire fucking life.

We kiss until I come dangerously close to fucking it all up, all over again.

Until she pushes me away, confusion and lust written in her flawless features.

"I'll sleep with Lina tonight and go home in the morning."

I don't answer, just nod at her words, and watch her every step as she walks away from me.

Again.

Chapter Twelve
Marco

It's late—or very early in the morning—when I step into Lina's room to find Enzo in the armchair, wide awake, staring at Lina like he's afraid she might just disappear at any moment. My gaze all too naturally slides over to the bed where River is lying on her back, her still-damp hair a sexy mess on the top of her head, wearing her favorite beige pajamas. Half of my walk-in closet still belongs to her and I refuse to change that. There isn't a doubt in my mind that she'll be back. The only variable is... when.

Every fiber in my body wants to keep her close, at home, where she belongs. But from the moment I inserted myself into her life, it's been a game of one step forward and three miles back.

"Tyler called me to bitch me out." I frown at Enzo's words, my eyes never deviating from the woman who has been consuming my every waking thought.

"How did he get your number?" Tyler and I are a lot alike. We both need control. We both have the means to have and keep that control. When he decided to get married to that ungrateful bitch, I warned him, but he was convinced they were in love. When she stepped out on him with his college buddy, who is also his business partner, I offered to put out a hit on them. He declined, although there was a second's pause where I thought he'd take me up on my offer.

But Tyler Walker prides himself on always doing the right thing. Underneath that hard exterior, he longs for the family he had before his sister died tragically at an all too young age.

"Fuck if I know, he's got almost as many connections as you. Hell, most of them are the same ones." The armchair creaks as he leans forward, his hands in a steeple.

It's like he's praying to the God he gave up on the day his deadbeat parents decided he wasn't worth it as they drove forty minutes to the Sisters of Life convent, dropped him off, and never looked back.

He was six. Too young to understand, but old enough to feel the abandonment. He rarely talks about his past and I wonder if, one day, I'll get the whole story.

River stirs and my instinct is to go to her, pick her up and tuck her away in my bedroom where she would stay for the rest of her days. Obviously, I'm not stupid enough to act on that. Barely.

"He's got eyes on her?" Knowing Lina, she figured it out and ditched them as easily as she lost our crew. Enzo scoffs and it's all the answer I need.

"He tried. Then blamed me for letting her get into a dangerous situation." I don't understand how he can stand by and watch her date another guy, knowing damn well he's been in love with her since they were kids. Before they even knew what love meant.

"He'll learn that Lina is impossible to keep under control." I told Tyler as much when I gave him my big brother speech about him hurting her and me breaking his kneecaps. Unnecessary since he knows me so fucking well.

"Yeah, but we'll go down trying." I have no doubts he will.

"Good luck with that." Approaching the bed, I use my pinky to brush away a strand of hair from River's eye. My knuckles are swollen, and even though I've iced them and the bleeding has stopped, the throbbing is a constant reminder of what happened a few hours ago.

Fuck, she's stunning. The slope of her nose is as straight as the steel in her spine. The bow in her lips is as sexy as the arch in her back when she comes all over my cock. Even with the blemish on her cheek from where that piece of shit backhanded her, she's perfect. But it's the green in her eyes that brings me to my knees every fucking time, and I'm grateful that I can't see them now or else I'd surrender to her without question.

I freeze when she stirs once more, only allowing myself to breathe when I think she's fallen back into a fitful sleep. Except she doesn't. Her breathing is shallow now. Eyes shifting behind her lids as she pretends to still be unconscious. Where her lips were slightly apart a second ago, they are now completely closed, her nostrils flaring just the tiniest bit more than when she slept earlier.

My *Tesoro* is awake and pretending otherwise. The lion in me roars, the chase palpable in the air, as my favorite prey tries to toy with me.

"Hey Enzo, you still got that chick in your room?" When he glares at me like I've lost my fucking mind, I smile and tilt my head toward River. Shaking his head, knowing damn well that our games never end well, he still plays along.

"Yeah, why? You wanna taste of the blonde?" I'm staring at River when he speaks, which is the only reason I notice the small tick in her jaw at his words. I'm a betting man when I know I can win, and I know for a fact that my next words are going to be the final blow.

"Why not?" River's eyes fly open, rage and jealousy like a living, breathing beast in those spellbinding green eyes of hers.

"Morning, *Tesoro*." I don't pretend I'm not toying with her and she's too smart not to realize it.

"You're an asshole."

"We've already established that." Shaking her head at my words, her worried gaze slides over to Lina, who's sleeping like a teen after their first all-nighter.

"She's fine, I promise. Come with me?" I extend my hand, my wedding band catching the dim light coming from the doorway.

I expect a fight, but instead I'm pleasantly surprised to see her looking at Enzo and silently telling him to take care of her before she places her small hand into mine, where it fits perfectly.

"Night."

Enzo doesn't answer me, except for a curt nod before he pulls the armchair closer and gets himself as comfortable as a big man can get in an upright sitting position. Always my sister's unmoving guardian. I can respect that.

Pulling River to walk in front of me through the door, I let her pass before I step beside her. My father may have been the king who sat on the throne of The City but he had rules—ideals he never broke—in this life where the law of the land didn't apply behind closed boardroom doors. There are three codes we live by. First, children are innocents, they are to be helped, not harmed. Second, revenge is served cold; always keep your emotions in check—clearly, I didn't follow this rule tonight. Above all else, he was adamant about the final Mancini law.

When you marry, you become two sides of the same coin. Twin thrones on a level dais. You walk side by side to show unity. Your rule is meaningless without your partner, so choose wisely.

River is my fate and I will burn this world down before I ever let her go.

"Did you put ice on that?" I can't take my eyes off her cheek, the wound more visible in this light, it's making my blood boil all over again.

"Yes, but I fell asleep pretty quickly so I'm not sure it worked its magic, yet." Without a word, I squeeze her hand and redirect our footsteps to the kitchen, where I take out a bag of ice from the freezer before rummaging through the drawers for a baggie. We're silent as I work and when I hear her chuckle beside me, I glance her way just as I'm opening the ice bag.

"What's so funny over there?" Fuck, it's cold.

"You looking all domestic and shit." Hmm, I love it when she curses. It means I get to fuck the filth right out of her mouth.

"That's three." Damn, I love playing this game.

"Yeah, yeah. You keep promising a punishment, yet here you are, putting just the right amount of ice chips in a baggie for me to put over my eye that some guy bruised up in a seedy nightclub. And by the way, you nearly killed that dude, so we are definitely having a conversation about that later." She scoffs, folding her arms across her chest and leaning her back against the counter, and all I can do is shake my head. She's right, I like to take care of her. Hell, I *need* to take care of her. But in the privacy of our darkest needs, I also need to see the marks I leave on her body while I make her come.

I don't see why it's so complicated.

"Is that your way of asking for permission?" Three more ice chips in the bag and I close it up tight to make sure any melted water doesn't leak.

"Please." It's her turn to shake her head in disbelief. "You want me to ask you for permission to punish me for using"—she air quotes her words here—"curse words around you?" It's her laughter that makes my cock impossibly hard. But as she slides her eyes to me, she knows. She can see me slowly, meticulously, sliding the baggie zipper closed, then handing it to her with a smirk firmly planted on my mouth.

She knows she's in trouble.

"Yes." Snapping up the baggie, she places it on her cheek, our gazes locked and loaded. "Well, I'm not going to. You realize that I was the domme in my job, not the other way around."

It's my turn to laugh.

"I highly doubt Tyler Walker is the submissive type." I try to be nonchalant, but I hate that my childhood friend tasted and touched my wife before me.

"Well, no. That was different. Which reminds me. We need to have a conversation about this whole love triangle you, Tyler, and Nathaniel have going on."

"That guy must have hit you harder than I thought for you to say something so irrational." Pushing myself off the counter, I take her hand and we head straight for my bedroom. I like this side of her, where she doesn't fight me at every corner; this side that chooses her battles to get what she wants.

"Well, it does throb like a bitch, but I'll survive." Yeah, she knows exactly what she wants.

"That's four."

"A lot of talking and no doing, Mancini. Gotta tell ya, Tyler was definitely more of a—" And that's where my patience evaporates like Lake Chad. I turn. I bend. I pick her up over my shoulder. In under a minute we're at my bedroom door, which I close and lock before dropping her unceremoniously on my bed.

"Strip."

"Well, hello there, green-eyed monster."

"Tell me, *Tesoro*, do you like playing with my patience? Do you like seeing how far you can push me before I lose my fucking mind? Well, you got my attention, so you better take those clothes off before they end up as rags for my housekeeper's cleaning bucket." That little fox just gives me a wily smile as she crosses her arms over her midsection and pulls her tank top off slowly enough to make my already-hard shaft twitch with unwavering need.

"I don't usually like my men jealous, Marco."

Liar.

"You don't have *men*, River. You have me. Your husband." I knew I wanted her, but I didn't realize how deeply seeded my need to possess her was until this very moment.

"Yeah, I think you're right." She shimmies out of her pants and pulls down her panties while she's at it.

Good girl.

"I know I'm right." I only take off my t-shirt, reaching back and pulling it over my head.

"Why is that? Why do I feel guilty every time Nathaniel tries to kiss me?" Jesus fucking Christ is she trying to kill me?

"Do you remember what happened the last time a man who wasn't me touched you?"

She stills and the look in her eyes stops me in my tracks. "His blood was everywhere." Her words are whispered, like she's afraid of putting them out into the universe.

I can't lose this moment, this connection between us right now, so I straddle her and push her back, sliding her completely beneath me. I've missed her body next to mine. Her breath on my chest while she used me as her own personal mattress.

"That's right, River. I will destroy any man who dares touch what's mine." For the first time since we've been together, I kiss her with my soul. Not my passion, not my lust. I take my time, licking her parted lips, tasting her tongue as she seeks out mine.

Naked under me, she wraps her long legs around my waist and pushes her heels into my ass, disintegrating all space between her pelvis and mine. I allow her to set the rhythm, give her the baton to lead this moment, and to my surprise, she doesn't fall back on hard and fast. Her movements are sinuous, like a feline brushing against me and begging for love.

Love.

What a strange notion, a foreign concept to me. An ideal taught to me by my parents as I watched them take care of each other. My ambition seemed too powerful to share with another, yet here I am, gazing down on this strong, relentless beauty who has tried to walk away from me while I've done everything to bring her back.

"Why do you say these things, Marco?" This question should feel like a trap, like she's forcing an answer from me during a moment of truth.

Cupping her head in my hands—mindful of her wound—I continue gliding our wet lips together as my answer breathes into her mouth.

"I promised you the truth. In my vows, I promised you'd be my number one priority. Those words are me keeping my promise." With my thumbs on her cheekbones, I part her lips with my tongue and with every sweep inside her mouth I tell her how perfect she is, how strong and resilient she is. How proud I am to call her my wife.

Every moan and every whimper is like a gift. Her hands are at my waist now, making quick work of my slacks and belt, pushing them down my thighs as I watch her watch me. I know this was her job. I know, and it fucking makes me feral that she's done this a thousand times before, but in this bubble of time, in this private moment between only us, it feels like more.

Once I'm naked, she does some voodoo shit with her hips and suddenly she's got me in a position I don't often allow.

She's on top, her delicate hands firmly holding me down, her short hair a messy mop on top of her head and her smile worth more than every one of my physical possessions.

"Proud of yourself, *Tesoro*?" She knows I could dominate her from this position, but I don't want to.

"Bet you can't say you've bottomed a lot, can you?" Her pussy is hot on my straining dick as she rubs her slit over it like she's lubing it up for us.

"Can't say that I have, no."

"How does it feel? To be subdued?" I almost laugh at that, but then the truth hits me. Physically, I could put an end to this in two seconds. But in all the ways that count, it'll never happen.

"It scares the shit out of me." All laughter leaves her gaze, her teeth sink into her bottom lip and her entire body stills at my words.

"Do you want me to stop?" The vulnerability in her voice is like a steel knife to my chest.

"*Mai, Tesoro. Mai.*"

"What does that mean?" Fisting her hair in my hand, I hold her just inches from my mouth before I devour her gasp when I tell her.

"It means *never*. I never want you to stop."

I worship her with my mouth, my free hand playing along the skin of her back while she pushes out her hips and sinks onto me with ease and grace. We both groan at the hot feel of her flesh surrounding my cock, her pussy enveloping me like I was made for her.

"Marco?"

"Hmm?" I've never kissed a woman so long that fucking was an afterthought, yet here I am, burying nine inches deep inside my wife and I can't stop tasting her mouth.

Licking her lips, biting her chin. I can't stop touching her, digging my nails into her skin.

I just can't stop.

"If you don't start fucking me, right now, I might just die from not coming." This time, I smile against her lips, and without being told twice, I push her on her side and hitch up her leg high on my waist. My hand cups her ass hard enough to bruise just as I start pounding into her like this very moment is our only salvation. Because being with her is the only time I feel whole.

Pulling her head back, I trail my teeth along the column of her neck and every time she shudders from my touch, I reward her with a quick bite. It's when my mouth reaches her tits that I become a wild beast rutting on the woman I cannot ignore or forget. Skin slapping skin, my balls hitting her flesh with every thrust inside her, I feel the signs of her impending orgasm.

In this position, my pelvis meets her clit with every movement. I fuck her tight little pussy with my entire body, rubbing up against her, as our sweat-ridden skin slips and slides from the sheer exertion of it all.

I fuck her like she's my drug and her orgasm is my high.

When her nails sink into my shoulders and her head falls away with a silent scream from her parted lips, I know it's my turn to let go.

Her pussy milks my cock, throbbing flesh against throbbing muscle as she squeezes her orgasm all over me and I release mine straight up inside her. In a small, minuscule window of time, I wonder what it would be like to watch my seed grow into so much more.

But then I shut that shit down.

I can't think like this. I can't hope for the future.

Not until River Fox-Mancini is mine in the present and for always.

Chapter Thirteen

River

The smell of vanilla floats through my senses as I slowly come to. Opening my eyes, I expect to find Marco's steel-gray gaze boring into me, but I'm met with an empty room. It's a simple, yet masculine and understated space, with an ensuite bathroom to the right and a giant walk-in closet to the left side of the room. The wooden dresser and bedside tables are all a deep, rich wood, matching the frame of the huge, dominating bed.

Practically passing out in Marco's arms in the early hours of this morning after several orgasms wasn't the most ideal situation, especially after finally starting to take steps forward into my new secret-free life. It's not something I'm going to complain too much about though, I didn't really resist. I knew exactly what Marco was doing when he manipulated me into staying, and I knew exactly what would happen as soon as I stepped foot inside this goddamn house, and I did it anyway.

Lina was fucked up when we left the club, and yes, it'd be nice for her to wake up this morning to a friendly face, but let's be real... she has people here, and it's not like I'm her bestie. She can cope without seeing her sister-in-law the morning after a night out.

"Mrs. Mancini." Stefano's soft voice is followed by a light knock on the door. "Are you awake? I have your breakfast."

In the couple months I spent living here, Stefano's ninja skills at appearing from nowhere at just the right time never failed to amaze me, and they still do as my stomach is rumbling for food.

"I'm awake, Stefano. You can come in." Asking him to put it by the door or letting him know I'm happy to come down for it is useless. He's a persistent little man, and I love the obvious joy he finds in just doing his job. It's like he lives for this shit, and who am I to take that away from him?

The door opens slowly, and in walks Stefano, tray of baked goods and coffee in hand. The croissant smells fresh, and I'm not surprised. Today is Friday, which means Luca will have been in the kitchen prepping food for a couple days.

"*Buon giorno, Signora*. Did you sleep well?" He places the tray on the bedside table closest to me and sets about pouring me a coffee.

"Thank you, Stefano. I did, yes." Sitting up, I keep myself covered up with the dark-green blanket and smile as he hands me my steaming cup. I close my eyes and inhale the beautiful scent of fresh coffee, allowing a small moan to escape as I exhale again.

Stefano chuckles and makes his way to the door. "We have missed you." He then shakes his head with a smile and closes the door behind him, leaving me alone with my thoughts once more.

I should get out of here. Make my excuses and just walk away.

No, I don't need an excuse. What the fuck am I thinking? I'm not a prisoner here. I don't owe them anything, least of all my false excuses.

The croissant and jam Stefano left for me are delicious, halting all my current plans of escape as the pastry melts in my mouth. It's fine, a girl can enjoy her breakfast and coffee before doing the walk of shame. Although, he's technically my husband, and I still have fresh clothes here I could wear if I really wanted to, so I suppose it can't be referred to as a walk of shame.

Fucking stupid name for it anyway, in my opinion.

After pouring myself another cup of coffee, I take my time in the shower, using excess amounts of Marco's vanilla-scented products, leaving barely anything in each bottle. Yes, it's a bitch move and completely uncalled for, but pissing him off is my new favorite game.

Not that I'll be playing it for much longer. I'm hoping Marco's obsession with me will end when the divorce goes through.

As I throw on my clothes from last night—because I can't allow myself to fall into the trap of Marco and all he offers—I realize covering myself in vanilla wasn't my brightest move.

Fucking man dickmatizes me, I swear it. It's like he has this power over me that makes me subconsciously do shit I wouldn't normally do.

My phone buzzes on the dresser as I'm drying my hair—bonus to short hair is, it only takes a few minutes to dry.

CAG: Sorry about last week, Skittles. Can I make it up to you?

Nathaniel. I wasn't sure if I'd hear from him again after he found Marco in my apartment and they had that weird-ass stand-off thing. I'm still not sure how I feel about it all. But maybe Nathaniel will give me the answers to all my questions. Marco refuses to tell me what the fuck is going on, so why not ask someone else?

It all seems so sensible now. Like, why didn't I think of this in the first place? Marco has twisted my insides and made me suspicious of someone who has been nothing but kind to me, and that's not fair to Nathaniel.

Me: Sure thing. *winky face emoji* When and where?

His response is almost instant, and I smile at the thought of him sitting at his mother's bedside as he messages.

CAG: Meet me by that bridge in Central Park, you know the one *winky face emoji* Are you free today?

Me: I am

CAG: 12pm?

Me: See ya there

Central Park is literally across the street from here, and it's still an hour before noon, so I have plenty of time to make my escape and find somewhere for more coffee before meeting Nathaniel. I wince as I remember I'm wearing yesterday's clothes, but I'm refusing to use the things Marco has here for me, so fuck it. Arranging to meet Nathaniel in an hour in dirty clothes and smelling like Marco is the second thing this morning that makes me question my sanity right now.

I'm so close to making it through the front door, my hand is on the knob, twisting it open, when a light, sing-song voice echoes through the hall.

"You better not be leaving without saying goodbye, Miss Nightclub-owner."

Lina bounds down the stairs, looking elegant as always, even after a night out. I half expected her to be in bed until this afternoon, but she must have had some of Stefano's magical coffee. Her pastel-pink satin housecoat with matching fluff on the trim would look ridiculous on anyone else, but nothing Lina wears shocks me. The way she carries herself and her confidence in the clothes she wears is admirable. She doesn't give a shit what anyone else thinks.

Whereas I have been used to dressing for a part, wearing what is expected of me to make a good impression.

"I thought you'd be in bed for a few more hours. I'm meeting a friend and didn't want to make a fuss. How're you feeling this morning?" I smile and pull her in for a hug when she's close enough, releasing my grip on the now half-open door.

"My head's a little fragile, but Stefano and Enzo have been feeding me pastries and coffee all morning. I heard Marco ask Stefano to bring you breakfast before he had to leave." She's so dramatic when she speaks, one of those people who uses their hands and facial expressions a lot.

I'm glad I won't have to leave her behind when this business with Marco is over. Now that she works for me, I have no choice in seeing her again. I mean, I could have said no, denied her a job, but then who knows where she may have ended up? There are some sleazy clubs in Manhattan, and I can't stomach the thought of allowing Lina to step into that kind of situation.

"So, Marco's not here?" My insides are warring over whether I'm happy or sad about this, and the indecision isn't a feeling I'm used to. My decisions of late have been questionable, but they've always been firm.

"Nope. Some work thing, I wasn't paying attention. Enzo was holding my hair back and I had my face in the toilet at the time. I know, gross. Remind me not to mix my drinks next time. You wanna come hang out for a bit?"

Hanging out with Lina usually consists of Game of Thrones re-runs, and some bitching about her brother and the staff in her salon. And I have a feeling our next hang-out will heavily involve some discussions about her new job, Tyler, and Enzo. Or at least, it better, because this girl is as complex as her brother, and she's drawn me in hook, line, and sinker.

"Sorry, babe. I'm meeting a friend today. Rain check though, yeah? Because we've got lots to talk about." I raise an eyebrow and smirk knowingly at her, amused as red flushes her olive cheeks.

"Yes, yes we do. You sure you can't stay now?"

She's desperate to talk, but I also can't cancel on Nathaniel. *Can I?* No. I have to remind myself that he doesn't deserve my anger and suspicion. It's all Marco's doing.

"I can't. Maybe later though, okay? You could come over to my place. I'll text you when I get home." I could end up standing here all day. Lina is a talker and I'm a listener, so I need to go before I convince myself to stay. And staying has nothing to do with waiting for Marco to get home. Nothing at all.

"Sounds good to me. I'm going in search of more coffee, I think the last dose is wearing off. Love ya, babe." She air-kisses my cheeks and slinks off to the kitchen, no doubt to find Luca and the coffee machine.

Smiling, I lightly shake my head as I open the front door and step out into the brisk March air.

"*Signora*." Stefano's voice makes me pause yet again, but I at least have one foot out of the door this time. He scurries toward me from the kitchen. "I made you a fresh coffee, you're spending the day with Miss Lina, *vero*?"

Every time I try to leave, something tries to pull me back into this place I no longer call home, but the familiarity of it all is like a beacon I'm trying desperately to ignore.

"No, I'm meeting with a friend today." His face darkens a little at that, eyebrows dipping ever so slightly—anyone who isn't used to reading body language wouldn't notice.

"Il Signor Mancini informed me you were staying. Luca has prepared snacks for you and Lina for the afternoon." I know what he's doing. Trying to guilt me into staying. The fact that Luca has made the extra effort to feed me and now it's going to go to waste should make me change my mind. But I know it'll get eaten by Enzo, no doubt. The silent giant eats like a horse.

"Sorry, Stefano. Gotta go." I blow him a kiss and continue out the door, closing it behind me and not giving him a chance to reply. It's extremely rude of me, but I'm too close to cracking and staying here, and I can't allow myself to do that.

Ten minutes away from meeting Nathaniel, coffee in hand, I sit on the nearest bench and just take in the beauty that is Central Park. It feels like forever since I did any people-watching; enjoying the laughter, smiles, and whispered conversations of passers by.

Barbie Girl pulses out from my phone, full blast, pulling me from my thoughts, and I answer without hesitation.

"Hey, Polly. Everything okay?" Not my usual greeting for Polly, but after only signing the papers yesterday, I'm worried she's changed her mind or something.

"Of course it is, darling. We just forgot a signature yesterday is all. Can you pop by my hotel today at some point?"

My heart returns to its normal position, away from my throat, and I shake my head at myself for how paranoid I'm being about this. This isn't usually me. I need to get my positive head back on and start believing in the good again.

"Sure, where are you staying at the moment?"

"That Mancini Luxury Hotel in Soho."

I almost choke on my own saliva at the mention of Marco's hotel, but I pull it together to answer. "Okay, no problem. I'll be there in about half an hour, does that work?"

"Yes darling. I'll tell Charles to make himself useful and fetch us some lunch."

"Ooh, I get to meet the elusive Charles?"

"You do, darling. See you soon."

Ending the call, my smile quickly drops as I realize what I've just done. I'm now going to have to cancel on Nathaniel—something I've been purposefully trying not to do all morning—to head straight toward a place owned by my husband—the person I'm actively trying to avoid. My third dumbass decision of the day.

Hopefully Marco's 'work thing' has nothing to do with this particular hotel and I can avoid him completely.

With five minutes left before midday, I quickly make my way out of Central Park to find the nearest cab to Soho.

It takes mere seconds to hail a cab, and once I'm inside, I pull out my phone and type a message to Nathaniel.

Me: Sorry. Have to raincheck. Something important came up.

CAG: Can't say I'm not disappointed. *Sad face emoji* You busy later?

Me: Yeah, sorry. Girls' night in. I'll text you later though. We can arrange coffee.

CAG: Okay. Thinking of you.

I don't reply to the last message. Even though I'm giving him another chance because my own shit has played a big part in why I've been giving him a hard time, I still can't shake the feeling that I'm out of the loop. I had my chance to find out more by meeting Nathaniel today, but the universe had other ideas. Yep, the universe.

I'll get the information I need, one way or another. But first, I have more papers to sign and a Charles to meet.

Chapter Fourteen

River

It's been over a week since I officially—all dotted lines signed and notarized—bought Rapture and became a business owner that doesn't involve me pissing in the mouths of my clients. At least, I hope not.

Nathaniel and I have been texting, trying to meet up, but our schedules are doing a great job of keeping us apart. Not to mention this ridiculous weird feeling I constantly get when I receive a message from him, like I'm cheating or something.

I'm not. This marriage is only real in the eyes of the mafia voodoo traditions. Oh, and the state of New York, but whatever. I've been meaning to file for divorce, but just like everything else related to the men around me, I can't seem to get my shit together.

It doesn't matter because in less than twenty-four hours, I'll be twenty-seven and just like every other birthday I've ever celebrated, it's a two-for-one party. Kai's birthday is today, the day before mine, so at midnight, we'll take a moment just for the two of us. When we were kids, our parents thought it was cute, like a secret moment where we would make our wishes minutes before and after midnight. Like the passing of the baton. *Here, your turn to celebrate.*

No matter what is going on between us, these moments will always be special.

"I made gluten-free cakes for you both." Petal's disturbing announcement stops me in the middle of wrapping Kai's present in a cloth and tweed. We don't use wrapping paper, it's not eco-friendly.

"That sounds..." *Disgusting?* "Interesting." No one in the history of the world—who has a soul—could ever say mean things to Petal without feeling like a shitty person.

"You're such a bad liar. Although, to be fair, you did a great job for eight years, so maybe I need to reevaluate your skills." My head snaps to stare at her, my mouth hanging open like a fish begging for water.

"Did you... did you just burn me?" I'm shocked. Sarcasm is not in Petal's repertoire.

"Too soon?" And there she is, her knitted brows and her teeth biting her bottom lip scream guilt.

"Nah, it's all good. I'm actually proud of you."

"We're always proud of Petal. she's the reason the universe leans toward goodness." Ev sweeps her up in his arms and kisses her like a knight in...

"What the fuck are you wearing?" Oh, and that color is just... no. Hell no.

"Overalls, city slicker. You may be wearing shoes with red soles, but some of us work with the land." I don't even pretend to reel in the rolling of my eyes.

"I'm wearing my Timberlands, ya dork. And aren't overalls supposed to be blue? Because that sorry excuse for a green leaning on diarrhea is not doing it." I can't even look at him, it's giving me flashbacks of tequila and bong nights.

"It was on sale and color doesn't matter when you're up to your eyeballs in horse shit."

Petal giggles as he steals a cookie from the counter, and all I can think about is sanitation.

"Please, for the love of all the goddesses, tell me you washed your hands."

He grins like a ten-year-old, showing all the crumbs and chocolate through his teeth, then walks back through the door without answering.

"He did, I heard the bathroom sink going." Thank fuck my brother isn't a complete Neanderthal. "By the way, the cakes aren't gluten-free. I was playing a prank." Oh my Gods. Who the fuck is corrupting my Petal?

Drying her hands, she rummages through her drawers and comes out with a deck of tarot cards that she adds to the birthday table. As with everything, we celebrate our birthdays in the traditions of the Pagans—who, by the way, are at the origin of the whole thing—with tarot readings, homemade gifts, and crystals galore.

"How's your husband doing?" A secret smile sneaks up on me, but I quickly wrestle it down into a frown. Petal's question throws me for a loop though. I'm so used to lying that it takes me a beat to remember that I can finally talk about the drama happening in my life.

"He's fine. We had sex last night, but I'm filing for divorce this week." There, succinct and truthful like the gods intended our conversation to be.

"There is so much to unpack in that simple statement, but I'm going to start with... you had sex? Again?" Of course she would start with that. And of fucking course it's at the exact moment Kai and Freya stroll into the kitchen. I'm expecting a snarky response from Freya—it's her specialty—but several seconds pass and nothing.

I turn to make sure I didn't hallucinate their arrival, but there they are, holding hands like lovers. Although the expressions on their faces tell a whole different story. It's like they're in physical pain.

I'm getting answers tonight because fuck this shit. Those two being together does not spell normal and yes, I'm aware that 'normal' isn't a word I'd use for any of my relationships but still, this is next level.

Rapt, I watch as Kai whispers in Freya's ear and she shakes her head no. I haven't seen her in a while and I have to admit she looks exhausted. I wonder if she's started a new job. I frown, trying to think back, but can't remember a time she actually worked.

"Okay, so we have the cards, the gifts, the cake." Petal turns to Kai and cocks her head to the side. "Kai, grab an orange and the honey please, will you?" This whole scene feels like I'm a fly on the wall watching without understanding. Something's up, and I hate not being in the loop.

"Is everything okay?" I'm asking Petal, but I'm watching Kai and Freya for any signs that lies are being spewed within these four walls. Again, I'm aware of my hypocrisy, but this is a time for new beginnings. Birthdays so close to the Spring Equinox are always associated with renewal.

The no lies zone doesn't only apply to me.

"Freya's been tired so I've been giving her some herbal tea to fight off fatigue." Her words ring true, not to mention Petal doesn't believe in lies—they fuck with our auras—but I don't miss Kai's lack of eye contact. The fact he physically turns away from me as Petal answers the question, the difficulty Freya has sitting down without wincing.

Placing my newly wrapped gift among the stack of others, I ignore everyone and walk up to Freya, placing the back of my hand to her cheek then forehead. She's warmer than is deemed healthy, but she's not burning up.

"Are you sick?"

My question is met with deafening silence, the stray chirp of a bird outside louder than necessary in contrast.

"Fuck!" We all turn our heads at the sound of Everest yelling loud enough to practically set off car alarms in the street. Petal, of course, runs to the window, opening it quickly and asking him what's going on.

"We forgot the wood logs for tonight, babe. Tell Kai to get his ass out here so he can help me chop." Scanning the three of us at the window, he frowns. "What? Why do you all look like you've seen a ghost?"

"Well, it was a bit dramatic, Bear. Next time, maybe come in and calmly let us know." Petal blows him a kiss and closes the window before giggling.

"Every time he has an outburst, I get flashbacks to the night he broke his leg. It's awful." I hate that she has to live with that memory forever. Rushing to her side, I give her a big hug and squeeze her hard, just like she prefers, then kiss her on the forehead just like Marco does for me when I'm feeling vulnerable.

I mentally shoo that thought away because I can't be thinking about him right now. I can't allow myself to have all these mixed feelings days before I file for divorce. And I most definitely do not want him here to celebrate my birthday with me.

Because I most definitely am doing that. Divorcing, that is. Soon.

"You're so perfect for him." We smile at each other and from the corner of my eye, I notice Kai walking to Freya and handing her a freshly poured cup of herbal tea with orange juice and honey.

"So is someone going to tell me what's going on with Freya?" I narrow my gaze at her and, despite our pasts and our passive-aggressive shit, I'm worried about her.

"Don't be ridiculous, everything's fine. I'm tired, not dying. Sorry my life isn't as dramatic as yours." Until she opens her mouth and almost chokes on her pettiness. "I may be pregnant." Her words are aimed at me, her faux sweet smile like a hyena about to rip your flesh to pieces. When did she become so bitchy?

"Freya, don't." Kai speaks through gritted teeth, his tone clear and unforgiving.

"God, we can't even joke around here anymore." Cocking her head to the side, she seems to have enough energy to rally up her cuntiness. "I'm fine, River. Just here to celebrate my husband's birthday."

Bomb.

Dropped.

"What?" Petal and I gasp and speak at the same time.

"Goddammit!" Kai sounds far from being a happy newlywed.

"What? I don't know why we're keeping it a secret. They're our best friends." I almost laugh at Freya's bullshit excuse. "They're our family, Kai. They deserve to know."

"Dude, get your ass out here, man. I can't chop all this shit on my own." Fucking Everest and his impeccable timing.

"Coming." As Kai walks by Freya, he points a finger at her and mutters, "Be good." We all scoff at that, like she's the last person to hold her tongue about any fucking thing.

"As if." How was this human my friend once upon a time?

Freya finishes her tea and excuses herself to the bedroom to take a nap.

"Petal, I swear to the gods, tell me what the fuck is going on." On a sigh, my sister-in-law shows me the extent of her pure, loyal, character.

"I want to, River, but it's not my story to tell. You'll know when it's time." We stare at each other, her words telling me a lot more than she thinks.

Freya's sick.

Kai is married.

Everyone knows but me.

Suddenly, I feel awful. Like I've been so preoccupied with my own drama that I'm no longer in the inner loop of this family dynamic. Nonetheless, I can respect her honesty.

"Okay. I'll wait."

Nights in early March are still freezing, but Everest built a big enough fire to keep us warm, though not big enough that the fire department had cause to check it out. Dinner was fun—simple, healthy foods to help lead us into a simple and healthy future—and our cakes were definitely not gluten-free. In fact, I may be well on my way to a food coma state and I'm not angry about it.

"It's almost time."

My head leaning on the lawn chair, I roll it to the side and narrow my eyes at Kai.

"I don't think I can move. That triple chocolate cake with literal cherries on top is having babies in my tummy." Everyone laughs at my words but I'm not even joking. It's like my stomach is growing with every minute that passes by.

"You're the baby. Suck it up, buttercup. It's time for your special bonding time with your bestie." He's right. I can't miss this. Just like I would never miss my time with Everest during Winter Solstice.

"Fiiiiine," I groan, throwing my blanket off me and heaving myself out of my chair.

"Don't forget your gifts!" Petal claps her hands, eyes bright with excitement. This is tradition and we Foxes don't break those, ever.

Just as I bend to pick up Kai's present, the backyard latch to the wooden door opens then closes, startling us all.

"Oh! I almost forgot!" I guess not *all*, Petal isn't surprised in the slightest.

"Hope it's not a bad time." I freeze at the sound of the voice. My entire body warms in an instant and it has absolutely nothing to do with the bonfire or the covers, and everything to do with the man himself.

The words are polite, the tone jovial, but the meaning behind them is clear. He knows it's a bad time and he doesn't give a flying fuck about it.

"The fuck is he doing here?" I jump at Kai's words, they're too close, too venomous.

"No, of course not! You're still married, you should be here to celebrate." Fucking Petal. I want to throttle her and hug her at the same time. How does she always know what I need?

Wait. No. I don't need him here.

I square off my shoulders and stand my ground as Marco makes a beeline for me, his handsome face getting clearer and clearer in the light of the fire. Shadows dance across his features, his skin buzzing with the crackling flames and his eyes melting me with their intensity. He's like a spider and, again, I'm the fucking fly trapped in the web of all that fucking sexiness.

Goddamn him for looking so good. For exuding such powerful pheromones that turn me into some babbling teenage idiot every time he pins me with his lustful eyes. That's all it is. Sex and want. It's not anything else. Not the way he tunes out the entire world when he's near me. Not the way he finds innocuous ways of touching me, feather light, whenever he can. Not the way he fends off any and all threats with his mere presence.

"*Buon compleanno, Tesoro.*" Did I mention his Italian always brings me to my knees?

Reaching out, Marco pushes away a strand of hair from my forehead. The gesture is so tender, so personal, that it fills a void inside my chest I never noticed was there before.

"What does that mean?" Maybe if I concentrate on the concrete aspect of this whole moment, I won't fall down the rabbit hole of my own feelings.

His fingers follow the line of my temple, down my cheek and across my jaw before his thumb possessively rubs my bottom lip, his fist pushing my chin to the perfect angle for his waiting mouth.

"It means, it's the first but far from the last birthday I'll be celebrating with you." Then his mouth is on mine and everything, everyone, every obstacle and every doubt, flies away with my twenty-six years, leaving me brand new for the next chapter in my life. I melt, Kai's gift falling on the grass at my feet as my arms wrap around his neck and his hands splay across my back, like he's trying to pull me in closer than is humanly possible.

"Why don't you ever kiss me like that?" Freya's pouty words interrupt us and I have to blink out of my stupor.

When I look up at Marco, his victorious grin is one I've never seen before.

I know his cocky grin.

His mischievous grin.

His murderous grin.

But this one? It's like he's reached up and pulled a star from the sky, ready to offer it to me.

"This is for you." I give myself a little shake of the head to put everything back in order in there. It's obvious I'm losing my mind one horny neuron at a time.

"Thank you." I raise a brow at him when I see he's wrapped it in cloth and not paper. He shrugs, his gaze darting to Petal before swinging right back to me.

"I had a little help."

With my impatience driving me forward, I quickly untie the silk ribbon and hand it over to him. "I'm sure we can find good ways to recycle this." It's not until the words rush out of my mouth that I realize I've just left the door wide open.

"Trust me, *Tesoro*, I have plans." The confident, arrogant, and sexy as fuck Marco is back in business and my pussy clenches with the need for him.

"I bet you do, you sex fie—" As the cloth falls away, I'm left with a square, white box branded with the gold lettering of a big French jeweler. I gasp, my eyes lifting to find Marco watching me intently.

Petal's swiss clock chimes twelve times in the kitchen, announcing it's officially my birthday.

"Open it." He whispers his command, but there's a hint of vulnerability in his voice that makes my heart stutter behind my ribcage.

Lifting the lid, I have one more obstacle keeping me from my gift. The silver oval sticker holding the white tissue paper together gives way under my nail, exposing the most breathtaking necklace I've ever seen.

"Oh, Marco, it's... I..." I lift the pendant, placing it in my palm so I can see—up close—the details of the white gold fox with a diamond encrusted tail—at least ten carats—and a rose quartz body.

"It reminded me of you." There's that softness in his voice again, the little boy trapped in a man's powerful body.

"I can't even…" Why am I so speechless? Yes, it's probably worth a small fortune, but that's not why I'm having difficulty expressing my emotions right now. It's because he went somewhere and picked out this incredibly stunning gift just for me.

It's when he puts his mouth to my ear, his breath running along my skin as he speaks, that I realize this means something to him.

Like, something real.

"The rose quartz for the tint in your cheeks when you're flustered. The diamond for your guarded heart, priceless and rare. And the fox because I'll always remember who you are at your very core." He kisses me then, soft and meaningful. Then he turns the pendant over, the words "*Mio Tesoro*" inscribed in cursive.

"Marco, this is too much." I say the words I'm supposed to say, but I don't mean them. I'm already in love with this necklace. There's no fucking way I'm refusing it. I may be independent, but I'm not a fucking idiot.

Marco lifts the jewelry and holds both ends of the delicate chain as he places the graceful gold around my neck.

At the hollow of my throat, the chain meets and falls into a straight line, the pendant resting just above my cleavage.

"I love it, Marco, thank you." We kiss once more just as Kai's voice interrupts us.

"You ready, Riv?" Oh, fuck. It all feels like déjà-vu from when Nathaniel was here for Winter Solstice and punches started flying. How do I get myself in these situations?

At the sound of Kai's question, Marco stiffens for a fraction of a second, our eyes colliding and an entire conversation happening without a single word.

Steel-gray eyes dare me to walk away, and as much as I love his punishments for me, this is a battle he can't win.

"Look, we're having a moment right now, so do not ruin it by going mafia madness on me, okay? You have your—literally bloody—traditions, I have mine. Less blood, more talk." Shaking his head, he chuckles, but he's still not completely okay with the thought of me going off with Kai.

"Don't worry, he's my husband too. It's their birthday thing from when they were kids and in love." Fucking Freya and her big, fucking mouth. She sounds like she's helping but she's just trying to fuck me over.

"River."

Oh, he's seething. But so am I.

"If you can't trust me, then I need you to walk away and stay away."

We have a stand-off of Western movie proportions before Marco—who apparently weighed the pros and cons of this situation in record time—bows his head and takes one step back. His eyes though, are on me, wordlessly communicating a very loud and clear "*Mine.*"

With a smile and a finger over my foxy pendant, I follow Kai to our family spot where we do our talking and smoking. The place where we tell our truths.

I'm hounding him before he even has time to light the joint.

"Okay, it's you and me, Kai. What the actual fuck is going on with you and Freya? And I don't want any of this vague bullshit, I want the truth. It's our birthday." Exchanging our gifts, he sighs before lying on the grass, a square pillow under his head.

We open our presents at the same time. I smile at the picture of my brother, Petal, Kai, and me from years back, nestled into a wooden frame he no doubt made himself. Our names are carved in the polished wood with intricate lettering and designs. It's thoughtful and perfect and I love it.

"Nice," he chuckles as he opens his gift. "Did you make it yourself?" It's a log carrier, basically a thick quilt-like fabric with wooden handles.

"No, I cheated and had it made by that guy on the other side of town. In my defense, my life has been a little hectic." We chuckle, but then I realize he's just biding his time.

"Fuck, Riv. Your life is like *Dynasty* on crack."

"Yeah, yeah. Quit stalling and tell me the story."

With a long exhale, Kai finally gets comfortable.

"We got married about two months ago."

"What?!" I'm shocked beyond reason. "I thought there was this whole elaborate wedding being planned."

"There was. I mean, there is. It's just..." He takes a deep inhale and slowly blows out the smoke from the doobie before handing it off to me. I definitely need a hit because this news is dumbfounding.

"Dude, just fucking say it. Clearly, Petal and Everest know, so, spill the tea."

"Fine. So, you know how her parents are traveling cross-country? Well, they couldn't afford to have her on their insurance since she's an adult so they cut her loose." I frown at this news. They always were a little flaky, but damn. She doesn't have a job, how is she supposed to pay for shit? Well, besides the obvious... get a fucking job. But this is a no-judging zone so I keep my thoughts to myself.

"Okay, but what does that have to do with—" Just as I take another toke from the joint, the pieces of the puzzle fall together and the full picture is crystal clear.

"Oh my God, Kai. That's..." I shut my mouth, looking around like the IRS is hiding in the bushes just waiting for me to denounce them. "It's fraud. You could lose everything!"

"I mean, they'd have to prove it. We've known each other forever, practically live together, so it's not like I'm doing something wrong." Is he kidding me, right now?

"Um, yes, you are. It's literally illegal. Plus, she could just get a job and get her own insurance." Then Freya's face from earlier, her fatigue, her mood swings—not that they're much different from her usual self—start to flash in my mind's eye.

"Oh, Kai."

"Yeah, she's sick, Riv. When she came to me and asked that I do this, I just couldn't say no." I think back to the night I heard Freya announcing their engagement, the look on his face, the fact he ran after me. It all starts to make sense.

"What is it? She's not dying, is she?" The guilt from calling her names in my head gnaws at me.

"No, she'll be fine. The problem was the medication. It costs a fuckload and without insurance or a job, she wouldn't have been able to get the medical attention she needed." *Fuck*.

I lay down next to him, making sure I don't touch him in any way. The stars are bright in the night sky and the chill is making me tremble a bit.

"What does she have?" *Please don't say cancer*. Fuck, I don't like her but I don't wish that shit on anyone.

"Hepatitis C."

Turning to look at Kai, I bolt upright and whisper-yell, "Please tell me you're not sleeping with her." There's no jealousy in my voice, only concern.

"No, it's not like that, Riv. We had to make it so that everyone thought we were really in love and shit, just in case anyone came sniffing around, but we haven't been a couple. When she does sleep over, it's usually because she's not feeling well and sleeps in the guest bedroom." I return to my lying position, the little buzz helping me to take this news in stride.

"That's why she's got that slight yellowish tint some-times. It's her liver." Little moments I couldn't understand before start to make sense now.

"Yeah, but the medication will help get rid of it all. It's a twelve-week program that we started a couple of weeks ago. We didn't want to start right off the bat, you know?"

"Yeah, I get it, but damn, Kai. It's risky." Then some-thing hits me. "So, you being pissed off at me for being fake married to Marco seems hypocritical now." I'm joking, but not really.

"Totally not the same."

"I beg to differ. But we can agree to disagree." Taking my picture frame, I get back up to my feet and wrap my blan-ket tightly around my torso. It's fucking freezing without the fire.

"Alright, I'm going back over there. We good?" Kai jumps up, picking up his stuff and shrugging at my words.

"We'll always be good, Riv." He comes in for a hug and, even though it's only in my head, I can practically hear Marco growling in my ear. A shiver runs down my spine at the thought of his possessive bullshit. I'm supposed to hate it but really, it fucking turns me on.

"You're cold." Yeah, sure. We'll go with that. What I am, is horny for one man and it's not my childhood love.

"I'm glad we talked things out, Kai. Your friendship means the world to me." I smile, but it only lasts half a second.

"We'll always be friends, no matter what. But, River? Make no mistake... you're my Psyche and always will be. It may not be now, but our time will come."

Chapter Fifteen

River

It's been a week since I turned twenty-seven, and I have spent most of it coming to grips with everything involved with running a business. Polly insisted on sticking around for a bit to help me along, which is a godsend because my limited schooling didn't prepare me for what a mammoth task all of this is.

Who ever said running a business was easy though?

I'm really enjoying the challenges it brings, but relying on other people to follow through with tasks like running reports on potential clients for the girls is not easy. I feel like I should be vetting every single one myself, just to make sure no one like the creep whose dick ended up in a box gets through the net. But Polly assures me that Sheryl and Lilly are now double checking each other's work—which is something they should have been doing anyway in my opinion. Though I understand that things were very different when Polly first began this business.

Mimi is on top of everything that happens inside the club itself, so with most things covered, it gives me plenty of time to learn the intricacies of all the moving parts. Between going through paperwork and policies with Polly, and getting to know all my new members of staff, this week has been hectic, and yet again, I've barely had time to speak with Nathaniel or even think about arranging a meet-up with him.

Although, after last weekend and my surprise birthday visitor, I feel even more guilty about making plans with a man who isn't my husband.

And yes, the show Marco and I put on in front of my family didn't exactly scream 'we're getting divorced', but he keeps pushing at every single one of my walls, burrowing himself deeper each time he surprises me. It knocks me off-guard and I become dickmatized by the Italian mafia boss that screams "red flags."

I don't understand why he's still pursuing me like he is. He has everything he could possibly want. His father's businesses are now his. If our contract hadn't been broken, it would have been over by now anyway, so I know he doesn't need me anymore. Maybe it's his control thing. I'm positive that if I gave in to him, giving him exactly what he wants from me, he'd get bored and drop me like a sack of bricks. Because then it would be on his terms.

There is something inside of me that doesn't want to test this theory though.

I'm not sure I want to be right.

After spending the morning with Polly, I'm ready for a chill night in.

As I step into my 'work' apartment, which is now my only apartment, I can't help but take notice of how fucking beautiful it is, if I do say so myself. The paint smell has completely faded, drowned out by my candles and incense sticks, and my new light-gray sofa is so soft I can't wait to snuggle onto it under a blanket. It was worth the lack of sleep to redecorate, and with several new locks on the door, it now feels like a home.

Pouring myself a large coffee with caramel creamer, I grab the freshly-popped popcorn from the microwave before settling down to find my first binge-watch of the evening. I'm trying to decide whether I'm in a romantic comedy or fantasy kind of mood when the buzzer for my apartment goes off. Rolling my eyes, because of course Marco would show up on my first relaxing night in too long, I stand and walk over to the intercom. I could've had the whole, fancy connected-to-my-phone kind, but that lends itself to hacking from a certain someone who *knows a guy.* And knowing my luck as of late, he'd find a way to lock me out of my own apartment.

Hang on though, if Marco was here, there's no way he would ring the buzzer from the outside. The last few times he showed up, he's been at my door, already in the building. Hell, he even waited for me inside my actual apartment.

Hmm. Curious. Who knows where I live other than Marco? Not my family, not Kai, as he only ever came to visit my old apartment...

Have I ordered anything I'm expecting to arrive today...?

Nope.

I'm wracking my brain as I press the button to speak to whoever buzzed.

"Hello?"

There is a small crackle before the reply comes. "Hey, it's me."

I can hear the smile in his voice and I instantly relax.

Nathaniel.

"Everything okay?"

"Yeah, just dropping by on the off chance you're available for a coffee?"

Technically, I am available, but I'm also already in my warm stars-and-moons PJs—despite it only being five thirty in the evening—and I've got a fresh coffee calling my name beside the sofa.

Closing my eyes for a moment, I sigh before pressing the buzzer to speak, resigned to losing some of my chill evening alone. At least a little bit of the guilt I've been feeling for blowing Nathaniel off will be eased if I agree to one coffee.

"Come on up. I just made a fresh pot."

He doesn't speak again and I assume he's now on his way to my door. I pad over and crack it open so he can let himself in as I pour him a coffee. The sound of the front door closing alerts me to his presence.

"Hey, Skittles. That coffee for me?"

Spinning round, coffee in hand, I smile at the man I once had a mini obsession over. The dark-gray T-shirt he's wearing hugs his body beautifully, showing off forearms worthy of being put in the spank-bank. But they're not in mine. No, *my* spank-bank is full of forearms covered in throbbing veins and dark hair and a cross tattoo inter-twined with roses and thorns.

But those are not thoughts for now.

"Yeah, one sugar and a little cream. Your usual." I pass it to him on my way to the sofa, gesturing with my head for him to follow instead of standing so awkwardly. It's so unlike him, but I guess he's never been here before, so maybe that's it.

I sit with my legs underneath me and grab my own coffee, bringing it to my mouth with both hands for a sip. There's a perfect temperature to enjoy coffee and I don't want to miss it. Nathaniel joins me, sitting with his hands around his own mug resting on his knees and avoiding eye contact.

The jovial attitude he entered with has fast disappeared and it seems like he has something on his mind. Maybe it has something to do with his mom?

"How's your mom doing?" I figure it's best just to ask. It seems shitty of me to try and move the conversation on quickly, but the sooner we can finish our coffee and I can get on with my evening alone, the better. And it's clear from his body language that Nathaniel wants to talk.

My Rose mask slides into place and my mind goes into work-mode. I'm helping a client.

Only, Nathaniel isn't a client, he never was, and this won't include any sexual activities.

"You're straight to the point, aren't you? I guess I shouldn't expect anything less." He chuckles, his shoulders gently bouncing up and down as he turns his head to me. "I need to tell you something."

"Oookay, wh—"

"You should forget about Marco. H—"

"Now wait a minute, Nathaniel. I won't have you coming into my apartment and telling me what I should and shouldn't be doing. Whatever is going on with Marco is my business, and mine alone." I'm trying to contain the burst of anger heating up my insides at the audacity of him, so I take a deep breath and raise a single eyebrow in challenge. Taking a sip of my coffee, I wait for his response, watching his face transform from agitated to soft, more like the Nathaniel I'm used to.

"Sorry, Skittles. Don't worry, I completely understand." He gives a tight smile and places his own coffee on the table in front of us.

But *does* he understand? The usual vibes he tends to give off aren't what's going on right now, it's like he's full of an energy I can't place.

"Do you wanna watch a movie with me?" Lightening the mood may be what is needed, so I can sacrifice some of my evening to make sure my friend is okay. Because that's what he is right now. A friend in need. Petal would have my hide for turning him away right now.

"Yeah, I'd love to." His shoulders drop slightly, as if some of the tension he's been holding onto has loosened.

We settle in on either side of the sofa and decide on a couple episodes of the new sci-fi series people have been raving about. I've got to say, it was a great choice. The main guy has a voice that oozes pure sex and I'm here for it. If I was alone, this would be an ideal time to pull a toy out of my bedside drawer, but I'm not.

Nathaniel has been quiet the whole time, his eyes fixed on the TV on the wall in front of us. I'm a couple of coffees in and now debating the switch to hot chocolate so I can get a good night's sleep, and Nathaniel's first coffee sits cold and untouched on the table.

As the credits roll for the end of the second episode, I stretch my arms out and yawn loudly, trying to give the hint that I'm getting tired and the evening has run its course. Nathaniel may have been quiet, but his knee stopped bouncing and his aura has been relaxed, so I'm hoping a night like this is all he needs.

"Thanks for the visit, Nathaniel. It's been great to have some company, but I think I'm going to head off to the land of dreams shortly."

He's slowly nodding his head as he rolls his shoulders forward and rests his hands between his knees.

"It really has been great. When I'm with you like this, everything else seems insignificant."

Fuck, this is my fault. I've allowed him to believe something could still happen between us, but what I once thought could be love was nothing more than an extreme lust for a wonderful man. He's just not the right man for me.

"Na—"

"Let me explain, Skittles." His smile feels more genuine now as he makes eye contact with me for the first time this evening. "When my dad died, my mom was angry. I could never understand the anger until my wife died, and then it consumed me."

"You don't have to—"

"It's fine. You need to know everything." He turns on the sofa to face me, one knee bent up with an arm rested there. "Before we met, officially, I was intent on finding an outlet for my anger. My mom had this whole plan to avenge my dad's death, and at the time, I thought it was a great idea."

He pauses, and my mind is reeling with what his mom could possibly have cooked up. It sounds crazy, and yet, with everything I've gone through lately, I'm not really surprised by his words.

"Then Tyler got involved."

"Wait, what?" My attention is immediately piqued, and it seems that I'm finally about to get some answers to the questions plaguing my mind. It's now that I remember Lina's drunken ramblings about Tyler being Nathaniel's wife's brother, and I wish that put some of the puzzle pieces together, but it doesn't. Yet.

"I told them about what my mom wanted, hoping they would understand and help. Instead, they told me I was being a psychopath. Can you believe that? Marco Mancini, a mafia boss who kills people for fun, told *me*, a doctor who saves lives, that I was a psychopath! They refused to help, so I had to take matters into my own hands. Then Tyler stuck his Goddamn nose in and hired you, so I had to move my plan forward." He pauses again, as if searching for the right words.

All he's doing right now is confusing the fuck out of me. Like, what the fuck was he planning that was so horrible, and what does it have to do with me? I can't make sense out of the information I'm being given, so I sit in silence, waiting for him to continue his strange-ass little story.

"After my dad committed suicide in his office at home, my mom found him. It destroyed her, and she told me about the woman he had been seeing, the reason he's no longer with us, and that he felt so guilty at betraying my mom he took his own life in penance."

Nathaniel is flip-flopping between subjects, and it's really not helping my confusion or how one thing matches up to the other. Maybe I have my dumb-bitch mode on right now and I'm just not seeing what's right in front of me.

"After refusing to help me, Tyler was the last person I expected to find with you, though I have reason to believe it was under orders. Then it all stopped and that was my chance. It was near-on impossible with Tyler taking up most of your time. Then I got to know you, and being with you calmed my thoughts. It was easy to get lost in the idea of you and my anger was just gone." He runs his hands through his hair, his palms flat on his head as his fingers curl, like he's trying to rein himself in. "I thought, there's no way she's responsible for this. She's too good. Until I caught you with that hippy freak you call a best friend."

What the fuck am I responsible for?

The air begins to turn sour and Nathaniel's energy starts coiling around him in agitation. His brows furrow, and his eyes glass over, unfocused. I go to speak, because this is just getting fucking weird now and I think this kind of conversation is best had in a public place. Somewhere I don't feel enclosed and trapped. But Nathaniel stops me, leaning forward and placing a hand over my mouth.

"Shh. Don't apologize, I know you didn't mean it."

Excuse me? I absolutely was not about to apologize. My eyes widen in some kind of warning, my brows going with them, hoping Nathaniel gets the hint and removes his hand from my face.

"Where was I?" He looks to the ceiling briefly before returning his gaze to mine. "Oh yeah, so then Marco went and got involved, laying this ridiculous claim over you. *Don't touch my princess or I'll fucking kill you, Reed.* Can you believe he actually said that? I mean, how dare he treat you like his property?"

At this point, he removes his hand from my mouth and cups my cheek, and despite the crazy falling from his lips, he looks just like the sweet, kinky guy from before. Shaking my head free, I stand and walk to my front door.

"Nathaniel, I think it's time for you to leave."

I'm not getting the answers I thought I would, and despite all the questions I still have, I'm too uncomfortable to continue this weird-ass conversation.

The change in Nathaniel happens almost in an instant, the sweet guy transforming into something darker, and not the kinky kind this time. Rising from the sofa, his features menacing, he prowls toward me, like a hunter sizing up his prey. I'm frozen in place by his transformation, and before I have time to realize what's going on, he rushes me, slamming my shoulders back against the wall, caging me within his arms.

"Nathaniel, wh—"

"Skittles, baby, why would I leave? It's me and you now. We're meant to be together. Fuck everyone else. We can move, go anywhere in the world. Yeah, just me and you."

He rubs himself up against me as he speaks, and with my arms trapped by my sides, it's almost impossible to get out of his grip.

"No, this can't and won't happen. I'm saying no, Nathaniel."

It's like he can't hear me as he continues to rub his crotch against me, his hard length on my lower stomach. All it does is make me feel sick. This is Nathaniel, I know he's into a bit of the kinky stuff and loves a chase, but I'm clearly not consenting to this.

"That's it, struggle a little, River." He punctuates his sentence with lips on mine, hard and bruising as he tries to force his tongue inside my mouth.

"I said no, Nathaniel," I manage to mumble, all while trying to keep my lips tightly sealed shut. But it's like he's in a trance, his mind elsewhere and his tunnel vision on getting what he needs from me.

"Come on, you fucking love it. You don't become a whore without loving this, River. I remember how wet you were when I chased you through the woods."

A surge of anger rushes from inside me. I'm in my own space, yet again, and I'm in a position that I really don't want to be in. The violation of the whole situation causes me to remember the guy who mutilated me here. Then I remember seeing his dick in a box, and the alleyway, and Frank... and Mr. Bobby. Then the guys from the night out with Lina flash into my mind, and the way Marco left the club covered in blood.

"Get. The fuck. Off me." Kneeing him in the balls is probably not the best thing I could have done, but it's the easiest way to stop a man in his tracks.

His hold on me loosens and he grabs his dick, then looks at me with something sinister in his eyes.

"Fine. If that's the way you want to play it, I suppose my mother is right. Once a whore, always a whore. You don't want it unless I'm paying for it, yeah? Do we need a contract to detail how I'm going to ruin your fucking pussy so badly that you bleed out?" Laughing, he pins me to the wall again, hands on my wrists beside my head, and slams his lips to mine once more.

This time, I open my mouth, his body is pressed too tightly against mine for me to lift a knee again, so I bite his lower lip as he tries to stick his tongue down my throat.

He grunts with the pain, blood trickling down his chin as he backs off a little.

"Dammit, River. What the fuck?" He blinks and, for a moment, I think he's finally coming out of his trance. Until, that is, he wipes the back of his hand against his chin and sees the blood. "I knew you were uneducated, but I didn't think you were fucking stupid." A crazy, bloodied grin appears on his face, his eyes focusing solely on mine, and I know I need to act.

With as much energy as I can gather from inside me, I remember what Kai taught me and force my hands down to my sides, making him let go of my wrists. Then I use everything I have left to slam my palms into his chest, shoving him away from me so I can run, grab my phone, and find solitude in my bathroom until the police arrive. And I'm now glad I took the time to reinforce the door due to my paranoia, which is clearly warranted.

He stumbles back a few paces, and his next words make my blood boil as he steps into my space again, backhanding me across the cheek.

"Marco's never going to accept those pathetic hippy freaks you call your family. Do yourself a favor an—"

I don't know what his next words are about to be, but I see red, shoving him again and again to get him away from me.

There's an almighty thud as Nathaniel falls backward, his head bouncing off the wall before he slides down to the floor.

I don't take the time to check on him as I rush for my phone to dial 9-1-1. But instead of the noises from an angry man coming after me, all I hear is silence.

Fuck, he's unconscious.

I guess that'll save me from hiding in the bathroom.

Turning so my back is no longer to him, just in case he wakes up, my fingers hover over the keypad before I risk a glance in his direction. I pause, my breath catching in my throat as I notice the pool of blood by his head, then panic really sets in.

Chapter Sixteen

Marco

"*Tesoro*, I was just thinking about you."

It's barely past nine at night and it has taken every ounce of my willpower not to grab the keys to my Aston and brave The City's perpetual traffic just to feel her warmth against my naked skin. Despite what River Fox-Mancini thinks, I know her better than I know anyone else, including my blood relatives. The knowledge feeds my obsessive need to keep her safe. At the same time, my fear of losing her is even greater, which explains why I had my phone close to me, the ringer on at maximum volume, just in case she decided to fuck off with her independence and agree to be glued to my side twenty-four-seven. I'd fucking lose my mind if she tried to call and I missed it. Is it irrational? Probably. Do I give a fuck? Not even remotely.

"Marc—" Her voice hitches like she can't breathe, her words watery like someone who has been crying for years. "I-I don't... I can't... it all happened so fast."

I'm out of my seat and running down the hall to my sister's bedroom, knowing damn well Enzo is in there with her. I don't know why I need him, but my gut is ruling my actions while my mind is trying to get to River as quickly as humanly possible.

"Baby, I need you to slow down. Take a breath and tell me what happened." My voice is calm because that's what River needs right now, but my pulse is racing like a thoroughbred at the gate. Banging on the door, vaguely aware of noises a big brother should never have to hear coming from his little, innocent, sister, I call out for Enzo with our emergency code. A code red.

"*Codice Rosso!*"

On the other end of the line, River takes in big gulps of air and with every inhale my heart sinks with fear. This, right here, is the reason I never gave a fuck about anyone outside my family. This debilitating panic I'm trying to subdue into nothingness grips me at my throat every time she hiccups.

"Breathe, *Tesoro*. Tell me what happened." In my office, I make a beeline for the safe, shaky fingers inputting the eight-digit code so I can get my gun. "I'm on my way, baby, talk to me." Flying down the stairs, I run across the white marble floors, making it to the front entrance in record time. Lina is at the top of the stairs yelling at me about something, but I can't answer her because I'm too concentrated on every word that tries to leave River's mouth.

"He just showed up. We talked and he was... oh God, Marco. He was just... not like him. I should have known. I should have done someth—" That last word ends on a sob, like the idea of whatever the fuck and whoever the fuck happened is too much for her to bear.

Suddenly, my fear is replaced by red, hot rage. The kind I only let myself feel when it concerns my wife's safety.

"I'm in the car, *Tesoro.* I'm on my way to you. Do not fucking move, do you understand me?"

Just as I press the button to turn the car on, Enzo flies into the passenger seat. I don't look at him, my concentration strictly on my driving as I hand him my phone. I don't need to tell him why, he knows what to do. In less than twenty seconds, River's cries and panic echo inside the cabin of my car. She's spiraling—a rarity for her—and I'm not sure what to do about it. River is the most self-controlled person I know, myself included.

"Who was at the apartment, *Tesoro*?"

Driving in Manhattan is every New Yorker's cross to bear. We live in the most incredible city in the world and the price we pay for it is this motherfucking endless stream of bumpers. I'm weaving in and out, ignoring the honks and middle fingers from every person I pass. It's either that or I'm shooting my way down 5th Avenue, killing every motherfucker who tries to slow me down. When I cut across to Fifty-Seventh, some asshole is double parked, warning lights flashing like a fucking beacon for me to run straight into him.

"River, it's Enzo. Who was in the apartment?"

I need to concentrate on the road, I'm no good to her dead. Just as the guy opens his driver's side door to get out, I slam my hand on the horn and barely have time to swerve to the left to avoid him. The added bonus is seeing him jump two stories from the fright. Fucking idiot.

"It was..." Her gulp is so loud I feel it on my skin. "Nath—Nathaniel."

Two seconds.

Our brains are the most extraordinary natural computers in the universe. We're not aware of its complexities, the speed at which they are capable of analyzing a situation and assessing all possible avenues.

Case in point, the span it takes for me to hear the name and the moment my hand flies to the steering wheel, beating it within an inch of its life, it takes exactly two seconds.

In that time, Nate's face flashed in my mind. Blood and guns. Knives, maybe. Did he beat her? Did he kidnap her? Is this a ransom call? Where the fuck is he? Why isn't he the one calling me? Did he rape her? Leave her for dead?

With every scenario, my blood boils to the point my skin physically burns. In those two seconds, I've taken a knife to his throat and severed his fucking head.

"Fuck, watch out!" My right hand quickly puts the gear shift in first as both my feet slam on the clutch and brakes at the same time. Tires screech and our bodies shoot forward. Thank fuck for seatbelts. I hadn't even realized I'd buckled in until the weight of it sears my chest.

The group of twenty-somethings jaywalking flip me off and I swear to Jesus, Mary, and the Holy fucking Spirit that if I wasn't racing against New York City traffic, I'd jump out of this car and rip their fingers off.

"What do I do, Marco? There's so much... blood." The shock of whatever he did is slowly giving way to panic. "Do I call the police?"

"Fuck." Enzo's curse only jacks up my fear even more.

Thankfully, once I'm on Second Avenue, the road is clear. Or as clear as it gets here in Manhattan. My eyes are darting all over the fucking place making sure obstacles aren't randomly being thrown at me.

"No!" Enzo and I both scream that one word at the same time. "Wait for me. Where are you bleeding? Where does it hurt?" I can't lose her. I refuse to fucking lose her.

As soon as I reach her apartment building—the longest nineteen minutes of my fucking life—I jump out, knowing damn well Enzo will take care of parking and join me as fast as possible. If she answers my question, I don't hear it, I'm already at her front entrance.

Any guilt I may have felt from invading her privacy and ordering copies of her keys disappears instantly. I made them for this reason, right here. Access to her. Immediate fucking access to her in case she can't make it to me.

I burst into her apartment, my gun pointed straight ahead, the space eerily quiet except for the hiccupped breathing coming from the wall just right of the entrance. I can't see her, can't look at her, but I slowly inch my way to her as my gun points to the body half propped up on the wall, one leg folded with both arms on the floor, limp.

"You okay, *Tesoro*?" My eyes scan Nate's body, mixed feelings invading my chest as the possibility of having lost one of my oldest and closest friends is laid out before me. My gaze lands on the pool of blood dripping from his shoulder and landing on the carpet.

That's going to be a bitch to clean.

Darting my eyes to River, I scan her body for any and all injuries, making sure she's not hurt or in need of an ambulance before I walk over to Nate and crouch at his side. He's unconscious but I can see his chest slowly rising and falling with every breath he takes in.

"What happened, *Tesoro*?" I'm afraid this might send River over the fucking edge. I may be used to blood and death, but this is a lot for her in such a short time. Most importantly, she needs to know that no matter the circumstances, I will always have my wife's back. Guilty or not.

"I don't... I don't know. He was... and then I just pushed and..."

"How long before you called me?" I'm using my calm voice, although I feel anything but at this point. The logical thing to do would be to call the police and the ambulance, do this above board, because disposing of Nathaniel Reed's body like some two-bit criminal nobody would notice missing is not the smart thing to do.

"I... don't know. A minute? May-maybe two?"

Nate's eyes blink open, unfocused and glassy with tears. I have no idea what happened here but I'm guessing whatever it was, River acted in self-defense, judging from the mark on her cheek. What is it with these assholes trying to hurt my wife?

Tyler and I knew Nate had a plan, but we thought we'd averted the situation when we intervened. We thought by keeping her to ourselves we were protecting him from himself. From his psycho mother. We were all like brothers, but Mr. Reed's death just flipped a switch in Eleonor's mind, like his suicide was an insult to her.

But Nate? His sanity evaporated the day Angelica died. That whole shitshow did him in and was the reason Tyler washed his hands of him. It was either that or kill him with those same hands.

When Nate came asking for our help to fuck with River, get her emotions all riled up and then dump her in the Hudson, Tyler and I decided we needed a plan. We tried talking him down, but we knew his mother was feeding his delusions. Keeping a constant eye on him, we made sure he wasn't a danger to anyone—including himself. Everything was going along perfectly until we lost track of him and I had Enzo take a look into River's situation, her past, her family, her schedule. I wanted to know everything so we could make sure Nate didn't do something he'd regret. That's when we found him living his new life in Midtown.

When it truly mattered, we tried being there for him.

Until, that is, I fell in love with River. Her true self. The real woman behind the name.

"I didn't want to hurt her." Nate's words are barely whispered, but loud enough to make River gasp. "I love her, Mancini." Blood is running down the side of his neck, his eyes unfocused as he tries to move them toward River's approaching form.

"Nathaniel, I'm so sorry. I'm so sorry. I didn't mean… you just… I said no. I said no. I kept saying no." My head slowly turns toward River, tear tracks running down her face like a stream of pain and memories that will never disappear.

Nostrils flaring like a fucking wolf on the hunt, I narrow my steely gaze on the man who was once my chosen brother. The kid who taught me how to observe the rich guys and read their tells. The boy who swore his undying love to his best friend's sister the day he slid a ring on her finger.

The man who lost so much in so little time that his mind gave up completely.

I should be trying to save his life, although there's not much I can do, but knowing he had his hands on my wife while she repeatedly told him no, that he tried to take away her dignity? Yeah, the man means nothing to me.

I wash my hands of him, his memory, his friendship. The brother I knew and loved died years ago, alongside his wife.

"It wasn't supposed to end like this."

His eyes close once more just as Enzo rushes in through the front door. My back is to him so I don't see his expression, but I'm sure I can guess. Shock at the scene before him, then he's all business as he inspects the room, the position of the body, and the different ways he can make it disappear.

"Take care of it. Fast." Standing to my full height, I give Nathaniel one last look, silently saying my final goodbyes. I don't know what happened to the man I knew but this version of him was damaged beyond repair. Maybe death comes as a comfort.

Enzo grunts his understanding, stepping in front of me with his phone at his ear.

"We've got a meat delivery order. Black Angus, fresh sirloin." Fucking hell, that man is missing the empathy gene... except when it comes to Lina, thank fuck.

"Come on, *Tesoro*. We need to go. Quietly."

River's eyes are fixed on Nate's still body like she's waiting for him to wake up. Except, what she doesn't realize is that if he were awake, I'd kill the motherfucker for putting his hands on my wife.

When she doesn't move, I carefully pick her up, all the while making sure neither one of us allows our shoes or any part of our skin to touch the growing puddle of blood. Cradled in my arms, I carry her over the threshold, and as I pull the door closed behind me, I hear Enzo's voice.

"The car is up Thirty-First toward Third Avenue."

I don't need keys, the door takes my fingerprint to open.

As River's body curls up tight around me, I bring my mouth to her temple and whisper words she understands. Words that will snap her out of this shell-shocked stupor.

"You will survive this. I'll make sure of it." Only when I place my lips to her skin do I realize she's not in shock. She's angry. Livid. Fucking pissed off.

At me.

"That's two, Marco Mancini. Since you've been in my life, I have killed *two* people." The venom in her voice is startling at first, but fuck it. I'd rather see her fighting than giving up.

"And they both deserved it."

Chapter Seventeen

River

My mind is reeling with guilt, pain, anger. *Mostly anger right now*. It's like the five stages of grief are all messed up and I've skipped straight over denial.

I know what I've done.

The fact of it is irrefutable.

But the anger... that shit, I'm holding onto.

Ever since Marco Mancini forced his way into my life, death has followed me like a bad smell. I'm not sure I can take any more, but I also don't think I have a choice. The fucking universe has got some explaining to do, because the plan it has for me right now feels like the least amount of fun I could imagine.

Marco tried to insist that I needed rest, to go to sleep and wake up in the morning with a fresh head, let him deal with it. But that's nearly impossible. Every time I close my eyes, I see the blood on my freshly painted wall, on my cream carpet... on Nathaniel's face as it drips from his mouth.

It was an accident, I never wanted to hurt him, but I also wasn't going to stand there and accept what was happening to me... again. So many *what ifs* are running through my mind, it's hard to concentrate on what Marco and Enzo are discussing in front of me.

Sitting on the sofa in Marco's plush office, the world is moving around me in a haze of horror as I listen to them go over tonight's events like they're talking about the weather.

"Ron has just messaged. The clean-up crew is finished in her apartment, and they're working on all the street cameras." Enzo's voice is gruff, and he completely ignores my existence as he speaks.

"*Grazie.*" Marco nods, then turns his attention to me. "We need to go over some things with you, *Tesoro,* but it can wait until morning. For now, you need to rest."

"Fuck that, Marco. Tell me now. Go over it now. Because after tonight is over, I never want to see you again."

It's only brief, but I'm sure I see him wince slightly as I speak. He's leaning back against the edge of his desk, exuding that powerful energy that seems to draw me in with merely a glance.

Not tonight, asshole.

He takes a deep breath before speaking again, and I catch Enzo glaring daggers at me, which I completely ignore, because he can go and fuck himself as well for all I care.

"Tonight, it is. Enzo, go and get Lina. *Grazie.* It's time she learned a little about the family business."

Enzo nods once before stepping out of the room in his usual silence, leaving me alone with my husband. Fucking *husband.* Some sort of shit that is.

Marco joins me where I'm curled up on the sofa, my legs underneath me and an arm wrapped around my waist, the other holding an ice pack against my face. Without speaking, he pulls me by the shoulders so I'm leaning into him instead. I don't resist. The numbness coursing through my body makes me want to crawl away and hide, become a shell of myself.

"Talk to me, *Tesoro.*" He's holding onto me like a lifeline, softly stroking his fingers up and down my arm, and I can feel him breathing me in as he gently kisses the top of my head.

The fire that burns within me is hot and cold, flaring up at intervals to protect me before shrinking right back down again. At this moment, it appears to be down. Along with all the walls I have spent time building over the years. *Goddammit.*

I don't speak, fearing what may come out of my mouth. Marco is a dick, yes, and the rage I'm holding inside for him wants to explode, but in this moment, he's helping me. In so many ways. I can't find my fight though. It has up and left, dead on the floor of my apartment. With Nathaniel.

Marco sighs, and I'm sure he's about to try again, but then the door opens and in walks Lina, followed by grumpy-ass Enzo.

As soon as she sets eyes on me, Lina rushes over, planting herself next to me and leaning in, so we're both practically sprawled over Marco as he continues to hold me. I'm now being held from both sides, and for the first time tonight, I feel safe.

"Oh, River. I'm so sorry. Enzo told me what happened. How are you doing?"

The thought makes me chuckle. Though, I'm sure being delirious is definitely not one of the stages of grief. How am I doing? Fucking shit is how. But I don't want to dampen Lina's usual light and sparkly aura, so I do what I do best. Fake it till I make it.

Sitting up—which is a struggle being surrounded by Mancinis—I plaster a tight smile on my face. "I feel like shit, to be honest. But I guess murdering a man will do that to a girl." The snark in my tone is hard to get rid of, so I shrug my shoulders before pulling in a wide-eyed Lina for a side hug. "Sorry. It's all just a lot, ya know?"

"Girl, I hear that."

"Okay, so we're obviously not getting the police involved." Marco is all business again beside me, but he doesn't move. He just stays there, with a hand caressing up and down my back.

Enzo sits in the chair opposite Marco's desk, his usual dark and brooding demeanor in place until I catch him tossing glances Lina's way. Every time he looks at her, I see a softness in his eyes. It's barely there, but I see it.

Nobody questions the decision to leave the police out of this, and I don't blame them. Knowing what I know about the Mancini family business—hotels aside—they really don't want the cops digging around.

So why did I call Marco, and not the police?

I don't fucking know.

It's done now, I have made my own bed and I must lie in it. However uncomfortable it may be.

"We are each other's alibis if anyone ever comes sniffing around. I'm sorry to have to include you, Lina, but the more of us there are telling the same story, the more believable it is."

Marco continues to explain what he needs each of us to do, what we need to say, how we need to act. And I swear, I am listening to every single word, but the disdain on Enzo's face when he looks at me is distracting. So much so, I can feel the warming comfort of anger bubbling up inside me again.

"What the actual fuck is your problem, Enzo?" I interrupt Marco, uncaring that he's in the middle of explaining important things I should be paying attention to.

Everything goes quiet, the only sound coming from Marco's hand sliding up and down my back.

"You should be listening to everything Marco is saying. This is all your doing, we are in this situ—"

"Enzo. Stop. Now." They both glare at each other in some ridiculous stare-off. "I think we're done for the night. Lina, *grazie, buona notte*."

My hands are shaking with unbridled anger as she stands, kissing me on the head before air kissing Marco's cheeks. "Look after our girl, big brother. *Buona notte*."

Marco's body beside mine is rigid, a low growl coming from deep within his throat as Enzo and Lina leave the office in silence. I've got to hand it to him; knowing my husband, he would usually have had his hands around Enzo's throat after the way he spoke to me—I've seen it before—but he seems to be restraining himself.

"Don't hold yourself back on my account, Marco. The situation is fucked already, what's a little more bloodshed going to do?" I'm being a bitch, I know I am, but around Marco, I can truly let go without fearing I'll push him away. He's like a boomerang, he keeps coming back for more.

"Enzo might work for me, but he is also my friend, and you're still in shock. Let's get you to bed and we can finish discussing all of this in the morning." He stands, his face hard as stone, and holds a hand out for me to take.

I don't take it.

Standing so that he's not towering over me quite so much, I square up to him as best I can.

"Friend? That's funny." I force a laugh. "Nathaniel was your friend too... apparently. He's dead now though, because you're all keeping fucking secrets from me and he lost his fucking mind somewhere along the way. And of course I'm in fucking shock. Anyone with a soul would be. Which says a lot about you, because all you're doing is organizing a clean-up crew and discussing how we can play pretend." I keep all emotion from my tone, staring Marco straight in the eye as I speak.

"I know what you're doing, *Tesoro*."

"Oh do you really, Mr. Big-shot Mancini? You know what I'm doing, yeah? What...? What am I doing, oh wise one?" My chest is pressed up against his now, and yeah, I'm practically begging him to throw me over his knee and spank my ass before fucking me into oblivion. There is no way I'm sleeping tonight without a huge distraction in the shape of Marco's dick.

But I'm too stubborn to ask for it. I don't want a pity fuck.

I need to forget.

Marco rubs at his eyes in frustration, taking a deep breath before setting those steel-gray's back on my face. He remains silent, as if a thousand options for what to do with me are running through his mind. I shouldn't be pushing him like this, the fucking mafia boss who could make me disappear without a trace. But at this point, I think that might be the better option.

Dying would be the easy way out, it would hurt less than I do now.

"Fine." I slide on the mask that is almost second nature to me, steeling my spine and brightening my features as if everything is right with the world. As if all I want right now is to please the man in front of me. "I'm going to bed, I'll be naked."

Reaching up on my toes, I softly kiss the corner of Marco's stiff lips before turning my back on him and heading toward the door.

Two steps away from my swift exit, Marco grips my wrist and spins me into him, where he is ready and waiting to lift me up and over his shoulder. I squeal as one of his hands tightly grips onto my ass as he opens the door and makes his way upstairs.

"We—"

"No."

Okay then… I guess I'm about to get the pounding I need.

We reach our—*his*—bedroom door, and he makes quick work of opening it and getting us inside. A sharp slap on my ass makes my clit throb in anticipation of what's to come. I'm ready to be dominated in a way that only Marco can.

The door slams shut with a loud bang and I flinch at the noise right before I'm unceremoniously thrown onto the huge bed I once claimed as my sanctuary.

"Come on then, big man. What now?"

"Now, you're going to stop pretending, and actually feel something." He looms over the bed, arms folded across his chest.

"What the fuck is that supposed to mean?" I'm at a disadvantage lying here on the bed, so I move to sit, positioning myself in a way I know damn well is sexy. Although… with the tears I have shed so far tonight, and still in my cozy PJs, I'm probably not pulling off the sexy as well as usual.

"I'm not going to fuck you, River."

"Oh no, what am I going to do? Mr. Mancini mafia man won't fuck me. My world is ending."

Standing from the bed, because it's fucking pointless sprawling myself across it, I make my way over to him.

"Do you feel guilty?"

His question takes me by surprise, and my mask slips a little before I pull myself back together.

"About not having your cock in my mouth yet… maybe."

I fall to my knees in front of him, reaching up to unzip his pants, but he stops me, grabbing my wrists and pulling me back to standing.

"I said, do you feel guilty?"

His eyes bore into mine, searching for fuck knows what. I don't try to break free of his hold. Instead, I stare right back at him, mirroring his intense expression.

A thousand words are on the tip of my tongue, but as we stand here in silence, our breaths mingling together, all thoughts of seduction flee my mind. The burning sensation behind my eyes becomes stronger, but I push that shit down harder.

"Yes! Okay? Yes, I feel fucking guilt, and shame, and anger, and... relief. And I know I'm a fucking monster for even thinking it, but I had to protect myself. I—"

"You don't need to explain yourself to me, *Tesoro*. I know your soul."

"Oh, fuck off, Marco. As if you do. I'm leaving. Get your hands off me." I feel like Jekyll and Hyde in this moment, my mouth is disconnecting from every other part of my body and running wild.

Pulling my wrists away from him, I back up. I don't actually want to leave, but I don't think I can handle the way he's looking at me. It's like he can see all my broken pieces.

"No. I'm staying right here. Always and forever. I won't allow you to run away, *Tesoro*. You can hit me, scream at me, blame me. Whatever you need, because you're mine,

and I'm yours, and we're together in everything we do."
He steps forward as he speaks, grabbing one of my wrists
again, and holding it up so I feel his heart beat beneath my
palm.

It's too much. I don't deserve his understanding.

Ripping my wrist away from him once more, I squeeze
my eyes shut and take a deep breath. On the exhale, I just
scream. Tears trickle down my cheeks and my hands clutch
at my head as I bend at the waist before my knees buckle
and I fall to the floor.

Marco is there in an instant, wrapping his huge arms
around me and stroking my hair. He doesn't speak, and
once my throat is sore I open my eyes. My vision is blurred
as the tears begin to dry and I stare, numb, into Marco's
shirt-covered chest.

After what feels like hours of just sitting on the carpeted
floor in silence, my body now curled into Marco's, he slides
an arm under my knees, the other at my waist, and lifts me.
He holds me close to him before placing me softly onto the
bed. I watch him undress, revealing his tattooed abs and
bulging forearms that would usually make me swoon. But
that moment has passed.

Now, in just his boxers, Marco climbs onto the bed,
lying on his side and pulling me into him. I go willingly.

"I'm sorry." My voice is just above a whisper, but I know he can hear me, his warm breath on the back of my neck.

"You don't need to do that. Not with me. You're always taking care of everyone else around you, forgetting the most important person... you."

I scoff. *What more can I say to that?*

"I mean it. Why do you do that?" His tone is soft and curious, no hint of the pity I fear.

I take a deep breath. This is the moment I'm typically supposed to let someone in, and I don't want to. Not because I don't want him, but because I do. The way this man has a direct link to my soul, body, and mind is scary, and if I let him go now, I might be able to piece myself back together eventually.

"Come on, *Tesoro*. Talk to me." The deep rumble of his voice does something to my insides, and all I want to do is open up to him, let it all out.

"When Everest was thirteen, my parents died. It was my fault. If I hadn't been such a brat about wanting to leave the party early so I could hang out with Kai, we wouldn't have even been in the car. Ev was back at the commune with Brad and Ginny, thank fuck." My voice starts out low and slow and I need a moment to gather my thoughts before I continue, so I take another deep breath.

Marco stiffens slightly but remains silent, softly stroking a hand up and down my arm.

"A car hit us at an intersection. Mom died on impact. According to the reports afterward, when the car hit our passenger side, she was crushed. Dad wasn't quite so lucky. The car spun and flipped over, leaving us hanging upside down, broken glass and shards of metal everywhere. Dad managed to unclip his seatbelt and crawled into the back to help me. I ached everywhere, but I was generally okay, apart from the shock. My parents may have been hippies, but their car wasn't a rundown heap like you'd think. They paid attention to our safety, always thinking of Ev and me."

Now I've started the story, it's like the words are just flowing, like they need somewhere else to go other than inside my head. I smile at the memories of Dad checking all the safety reports of various cars before settling on the blue Toyota.

"I remember there was a cut on the side of his neck, where I'm guessing the seatbelt had dug in, but he seemed to be moving just fine as he helped me. But then, as I was crawling out through the window, I heard him cough, like something was stuck in his throat. I turned to grab his hand, wanting to pull him out with me, but his eyes went wide, a single tear falling from one. I held onto his wrist and he wrapped his fingers around mine, unmoving, then just smiled. A really sad kind of smile. That's when he said, 'take care of your brother, because he's all you've got left. You're a Fox, River. Never forget that'…" I pause, the image is seared into my memories forever.

"He didn't say anything else. His eyes kind of rolled into the back of his head and blood trickled from his mouth, then he was gone. And I was alone, on the side of a road, in the middle of nowhere, with two dead parents. The other car had driven off, long gone. And if I hadn't made them leave the party early, then it never would've happened. Taking care of Everest gave me something else to focus on and I've been doing it ever since. I know he doesn't need me anymore, but I guess I still kind of need him. Letting him grow up means he'll leave me too, then I'll be alone." I have no tears left, but just admitting the words out loud feels like a small balm to my soul. Though I can recall every detail about the accident, the party and the whole day leading up to it have been erased from my mind.

"You'll never be alone, *Tesoro*. Letting your brother take care of himself doesn't mean you have to let him go. He's your blood."

The stroking up and down my arm stops and Marco pulls me around so I'm on my back looking up at him. He brings a hand to my face, his palm resting against my cheek and chin as his thumb strokes over my lips.

"And I'm not going anywhere. *Ti amo.* I love you, River Fox-Mancini, and there is nothing you could say or do to make me believe otherwise. I will hold you up when you fall and cheer you on when you rise. I will always be by your side. You don't need me, because you're a powerhouse all on your own, but that will never stop me. Never."

His lips gently press against mine. It's not heated or urgent or anything like how he usually kisses me. This time it's full of a passion I've never experienced, one I never even knew existed until this moment. I can feel every ounce of his heart and soul being poured into the kiss as his lips move softly, his tongue slowly gaining access and caressing the inside of my mouth. His hand moves down to my neck where his thumb continues to stroke against my skin.

I have no words as a moan escapes my throat when his fingers pinch at my nipple, his lips moving across to my cheek and down my neck. He continues to kiss and lick at my skin as he slowly lifts my top, his lips only breaking contact when he pulls it over my head.

Moving down my body, he removes my pajama bottoms before placing his head in between my legs and kissing each of my thighs all over. He looks up at me through lust-filled eyes as he slides his tongue over my slit, pausing to suck my clit into his mouth, then continues to trail his tongue up my stomach and around my nipple. The sensations and tingles throughout my body are too much and not enough, all at the same time.

He continues to worship my body, and I writhe and moan beneath him. His mouth finds mine once more, and I don't know when he took his boxers off, but I can feel his hard length nestled against the apex of my thighs, rubbing through the slickness his attentions have created.

Our tongues tangle together, neither one dominating, more like they're in a dance, each complimenting the other. Then his thick, hard cock finds my entrance and he begins pushing inside me. The guttural growl he emits sends a shiver down my spine, like a direct line to my clit.

Marco slowly slides all the way in, and I suck on his tongue as he pulls out again, pinching at my nipple before thrusting back inside me. He continues gliding in and out of me, hitting all the right spots every time he's fully seated.

This is different to every other time we've been together. It isn't just sex. It's so much more. Every touch, every kiss, every groan is filled with tenderness, with love, and I find myself getting lost in this moment. He grabs my thigh and lifts my leg over his shoulder, pinning me in place so he can push deeper inside me. An orgasm builds slowly, starting in my toes, creeping up my legs before coursing through my whole body and leaving me breathless as Marco's movements become erratic. With one final, hard thrust, he stills inside me and takes his time kissing the ever-loving fuck out of me.

Pulling his lips away, he rests his head against mine, our heavy breaths mingling together. I squeal as he flips us over so I'm lying on top of him, his cock still buried inside me.

There's so much I want to say, to do, to... I don't even know at this point.

But I don't.

Instead, I rest my head against his neck and close my eyes.

Tomorrow is a new day. There is fuck all I can do about what has happened, and like Rafiki says, "It doesn't matter, it's in the past..."

Although, it does matter. I—

Marco's whispered words bring me back from allowing my thoughts to spiral, and I relax into him.

"*Dormi, Tesoro.* Sleep, now."

Chapter Eighteen

Marco

I'm Italian, but I'm also American. The New World born from the Old World. It's not two warring identities fighting inside me; one filled with traditions and superstitions and the other of pragmatism and modernism. It's not how it works.

I'm the sum total of both.

I am the tornado of two eras working together and creating the man I project to the outside world.

Cold. Calculated. Controlled.

Strong and ruthless.

Heartless.

But in my home, in my bed, with my wife, I am Marco Mancini and I am none of those things.

Alone with River, I'm just a man in love with a girl he met at a time when life seemed so simple and my only responsibility was to make sure I had enough condoms on me.

As I lie here for the second night in a row, holding my wife as she battles with her demons—our demons—I allow my mind to wander back to last night, analyzing every word she said. Every memory she recalled. Every detail she exposed.

The party, her parents, the car accident.

The car vanishing into thin air.

In my thirty-two years, I have seen a lot of shit in this life. My family's hands aren't immaculate. They're drenched in blood so thick it stains the very fabric of our souls. We have our reasons for killing, mostly to protect those we love or destroy our enemies.

Which is why I cannot fathom someone killing innocents like River's parents, especially with a child—albeit almost an adult—in the back seat. It goes against everything we are and vow to be.

Her story only makes me want to keep her closer, protect her from anything that could cause her an ounce of pain.

Hell, I want to go Beast on her, and if I have to start calling her Belle while I trap her in my castle, I fucking will, as long as she's safe in my arms.

The only problem is River and her fucking stubborn streak.

Why does she fight me on everything? What is independence if, at the end of the day, you're dead?

I shudder at the thought of losing her, causing her to move closer, her body pressing into mine, until all I can feel is her skin from my collar bone to my toes. Every inch of her is touching every inch of me.

Reality begins to sink in with every second of the rising sun above the horizon of Central Park. The advantage of having an indecent amount of money is the privacy it affords. Even with binoculars from across the park, the exterior tint of my windows acts as a wall. Our view is exceptional while we stay hidden from prying eyes.

But I know.

I know I have truths to tell and secrets to divulge, but I cannot lose River over decisions made without my knowledge and, even less, my consent.

But you knew, asshole. You've had months to tell her.

Gritting my teeth, I shove down the bitchy voice of reason and search for my cold and calculating side so I can move forward with my plan. It has to be this way for everyone's safety.

"It's a new day." I grin at River's groggy words, sleep still stuck in her throat.

"That it is, *Tesoro*." Kissing her on the top of her head, I run my forefinger from her wrist, up her arm to her elbow, before skimming right back down to her wrist. I repeat the motion like a soothing ritual to remind me of why I'm doing everything I have to do.

River Fox-Mancini.

"It's Spring Equinox, today. We have to celebrate." I bite my bottom lip to refrain from laughing. I stopped counting the number of times I made my wife come last night. She practically fell into an orgasmic coma, yet the first thing she thinks about as she wakes up is the date?

Fucking hell, this woman will be the death of me.

"I'm pretty sure we started celebrating last night."

"We did? What do you mean?" I love that her voice is hoarse from how loudly she worshiped my cock.

"I remember you screaming and thanking God quite a few times between midnight and three in the morning. Ow!" She fucking pinched my nipple. "Woman, I will spank that ass fifty shades of red if you ever do that again. Ow!"

Circling her wrists with my fingers, I make quick work of trapping her beneath my body—chest to chest, cock to pussy—my mouth so close to hers I can feel her breath on my lips.

"Apologize, *dolcezza*, or else you'll be begging God to save you instead of making you come."

"And you're God, in this scenario?"

"I am the Father, the Son, and the Holy motherfucking Spirit when it comes to your orgasms." I punctuate my last word with my steel-hard dick sliding right between her pussy lips until I bottom out and she moans my name. As it should be. As it should *always* be.

"Ah, if this is punishment, I may have to pinch you every morning."

Right. I guess the spanking will have to wait until I'm capable of resisting her without fucking her into oblivion.

That day is not today.

Born and raised Catholic, it's no easy feat to reconcile River's witchy side with my faith, but if it means taking part in such an important part of her life, then I will act now and feel that Catholic guilt later.

"You know, I'd understand if you didn't want to come with me tonight." River's words earn her a side glare just long enough to be deemed safe while I'm driving.

"Don't say ridiculous things. You're my wife." She scoffs at my words, as though our marriage is still a farce. In an instant, my hand is between her legs, a quick slap to her pussy to get her thoughts straight.

"Ow! What was that for?"

"A reminder." Weaving from the right lane to the left, I push my Lamborghini Urus through weeknight traffic, earning a couple of road rage honks along the way.

"Of what?"

With a smirk on my lips, I glance at my wife and notice her white knuckled grip on my black leather bucket seats.

"That my hands were made to pleasure you when you're a good girl and punish you when you mock our marriage vows." A stream of red tail lights illuminate the Verrazano-Narrows Bridge ahead, making me sigh in disappointment. Driving in New York is only fun at three in the morning, anything before or after is the seventh circle of Hell.

"You don't play fair."

"No, *Dolcezza*, I do not. But you know this about me and still... here we are." Freeing my hand so I can use the shift lever, I keep my eyes on the road as we come to a stop, right behind some hipster in his electric car.

"See? Now that's what you should be driving instead of this environmental disaster you call a car."

I frown, her words like acid on fresh paint.

"A car?" We are officially stuck in traffic so I slowly turn to face River, affronted by her minimalist view of this masterpiece on wheels.

Confused, she looks around, then out the windshield like the information she needs will be written across the hood.

"Is it an SUV?" Fuck, this woman makes me crazy in all the good ways.

"SUV…" I mutter those three offensive letters like a curse. "It's a fucking paragon, River. Do not belittle her by calling her simple, mere mortal names." The sound of her laughter echoes around the cabin of my Lambo just as traffic fluidifies and the red taillights dissipate. I could drown in that sound, bathe in her happiness, especially knowing I caused it. It's better than any drug that could ever be invented and I'm the sole owner of it.

"She? You're ridiculous. And what the fuck is a paragon?"

I grin, even though she's insulted my baby, because every time she sounds carefree I feel as though I'm sitting on the top of the world with her on my lap. And when she curses, well, that's an invitation to filthy games in the privacy of our bedroom. I'm a winner through and through.

"It means perfection. Like a model of excellence, a flawless one hundred carat diamond." I take her hand, bring it to my lips, and whisper against her skin. "It's you. You are a paragon, Mrs. Mancini."

"You know, I'm a sure thing. No need to butter me up in order to fuck me."

"That's two, *Tesoro*, and you better believe you'll be paying up for that dirty mouth of yours on this night of new beginnings."

When we finally arrive at her brother's, I feel like I've driven cross-country instead of just over to the next borough.

"Okay, so just remember. They are my family and we have traditions—" I don't let her finish that insulting phrase before my fingers are around her throat and my lips are teasing her mouth.

"Trust me, I remember. But don't *you* forget that *I* am your family, too." Without taking our eyes off each other, I reach into the inside pocket of my coat and pull out my wife's engagement and wedding rings, placing them on her left ring finger where they fucking belong. The night she left our home, her rings sitting in plain view, was the night I realized there was no turning back for me, no matter the circumstances. However, if I've learned one thing about River, it's that her independence is essentially the core of her existence. I couldn't force her to put them back on until the moment was right. By the look on her face, this particular moment may still not be ideal.

I take perverse satisfaction in watching River's nostrils flare, her cheeks flush, her biteable lips parting like the fucking Red Sea. "Do you have something to add, *Tesoro*?" As I lick a path at the seam of her mouth, I hum my pleasure.

"Yeah, I do, actually." Her sass is making me rock hard and I feel like I might just lose this game of cat and mouse. "You're lucky you have a magic dick or else this whole alpha asshole show would be a huge turn-off." She has the audacity to throw me a fake smile before she bites my bottom lip—hard—and walks out of my fucking car. I wish I could say I'm pissed, but I'm not. I'm the opposite. I'm fucking proud to have a woman with a steel spine ruling this city at my side.

My hands in the front pockets of my slacks, I walk behind my wife with a grin on my face. We haven't even reached the door yet when it flies open and the tiny woman with long, flowing golden hair throws herself at River with a giggle as pure as a child's.

"Hello, Gorgeous! It feels like I haven't seen you in forever." River returns the hug while I stand back and appreciate the love they share.

"Hey, Beautiful. It's barely been a week!" River's words are muffled by the thick strands of Petal's hair.

"A week is too long, River."

"Not in New York traffic." The words escape my mouth against my will, but I'm not wrong.

"Oh, I see you brought tall, dark, and..." I'm waiting for her to say handsome since it's the logical ending to that expression. Instead, Petal's words trail away as she stares over River's shoulder, her eyes fixed on the road.

I follow her line of sight and realize she's staring at my car.

Here we go.

"Tall, dark, and environmentally unconscious, apparently." Before River, that gratuitous attack would have slid off my back and barely reached my ears. But now, a tiny increment of guilt settles at the forefront of my mind. Not because I believe my choice of vehicle will single-handedly destroy the planet, but because I realize it's important for River's family to accept me and welcome me into their home. Without them, I could never, truly, have my wife's trust and unconditional love.

"Oh, but Petal, look again. It's not a car, it's a *paragon*." River throws my words at Petal, whose face is now scrunched up and looking mighty confused.

"What's a paragon?"

Behind Petal, a large booming voice answers for me.

"It's like white aura, babe. The golden unicorn." Oh for fuck's sake. A unicorn? Really? "Hey, Sis. What's cookin'? Why are you guys standing outside? It's chilly." Now it's his turn to look at the Lambo and he has the decency to whistle his appreciation. Now, that's more like it.

"Bruh, you are a brave man to leave that thing sitting on the curb at night." My eyes widen in horror, my shoulders tensing and my mind whirring with worst case scenarios.

When his eyes slide over to mine, he grins like a fool and I realize his laughter is just the deeper, more masculine version of River's. "I'm just fucking with you, man. It's all good." Apparently, their love of curse words is another trait they share.

It's my turn to play a little. With a wicked grin on my lips, I take two steps closer to my brother-in-law and murmur just loud enough for him to hear me. "You know, most of the people who just fuck with me end up lost in the East River." I step back and watch his goofy grin slide right off his face as his eyes widen with understanding. Before he can have a coronary, I slap him on the shoulder and use his own words against him. "I'm just fucking with you, brother."

"Right, right. Well, let's go inside then." Taking my wife's hand in mine, I pull her close and kiss her cheek.

"You're an asshole, Marco Mancini. Now my brother is going to think you're some mafia—" she cuts herself off, and I can see the events of the last few days flash across her face in the form of emotions. Fuck. Goddammit! "Well, we did say we were going to be honest with each other. Doesn't get more real than this shit."

That's my girl.

"Three." I squeeze her hand and from the corner of my eye see her shaking her head in barely contained exasperation.

"Kai, man, can you grab the beers for us?" Everest calls out, and I internally roll my eyes.

This guy again? I should put a price on his head, may the best hitman win. Kai—what the fuck kind of name is that anyway?—walks over to us and barely acknowledges my existence, which only solidifies my opinion of him. He's a fucking coward and River deserves a man who will go to bat for her. Every fucking day. This clown? He lives in the bubble of his own insecurities.

"Hey, how are you? Happy Spring Equinox." I watch my wife as she interacts with her childhood love and notice the little things. Her hand is still firmly in mine, her fingers weaved tightly through mine. Her body doesn't lean toward him, but remains steadfast at my side, my partner.

"I'm good, yeah. We've got everything set up out back. Grab your blanket and join us."

It's only then, in the heavy silence of River's disapproval, that Kai finally turns to me and holds out his hand for me to shake. Oh, you spineless fool. I could use your bones as toothpicks if I didn't know for a fact it would hurt my wife.

But I'm the bigger man, so I do what I must and hold out my right hand as my left pulls River a tiny increment closer to me. It's enough for him to notice and to get my message. "I'm being polite, but she's mine." We shake hands quickly and he nods and walks away like a lost puppy who's finally been severed from his mother's tit.

"You're being an alpha asshole again." River's breath is at my ear and my dick responds in earnest.

"It's what I do."

"It's what you do, indeed."

An hour later, I've got a shovel in my hands and it has nothing to do with burying bodies.

"As the Earth's axis turns toward new beginnings, we offer our generous Mother the roots for a new year." River, Petal, and Freya are dressed in white, ankle-length gowns as they lean on their own shovels. If someone had told me a year ago I'd be standing around in a circle like a druid in Stonehenge, I would have laughed in their face. Yet, here I fucking am, about to make a hole in the ground and plant a fucking tree. Actually, I have to plant three, apparently, because I drive a gas guzzler. Petal's words, not mine.

"Before we begin," Petal's voice takes on a vibrant quality, as though the next thing she's about to say will forever change the lives of everyone in the circle. She reaches out and takes Everest's hand in hers and, with a nod to each other, she does exactly as I predicted. "We'd like to announce on this night of rebirth, that we are carrying life. New life for a new beginning." *Boom*. There's a collective gasp around the circle before everyone rushes to Everest and Petal for a hippie hug fest. I stand on the sidelines, not wanting to impose, when River's fingers wrap around my wrist and pull me into the exuberant show of affection.

Now, I'm Italian. Touching and over the top emotional outbursts are par for the course, but that's within the privacy of my own family. This is not that.

"If you're my family, Marco Mancini, then they are yours, too." As always, my wife surprises me with her candor and open heart.

I guess, this *is* that after all.

Except for Kai. That guy can fuck right off. And Freya? I'm watching her too, because I don't fucking trust her conniving little face.

After we all congratulate and express our best wishes for a new life, my eyes drift to River's belly, and feelings I thought were reserved for much later in my life make their way to the surface. It's when I reach her eyes—filled with mirth and mischief—that I realize she's not there yet.

"Don't even think about it, Mancini. This belly ain't bearing shit for a while." Fuck, the way she's able to read my mind turns me the fuck on.

It takes us over an hour to plant a tree—three for me—and voice our wishes for the spring of our lives. I go with health for all while everyone else has elaborate wishes for planet Earth. The cynic in me wants to tell them they're all wishing upon a dead star, but it's not the place and definitely not the time to burst their hippie bubble.

I've got River sitting on my lap, the fire blazing hot enough to keep us warm and cozy, when the doorbell rings. We all look at each other before my eyes fall on my wrist to check the time on my Rolex.

It's almost eleven at night. Who the fuck comes knocking this late unless it's to announce something terrible?

My hackles are up, my senses telling me this is not good while my instincts have only one goal... Protect River at all costs.

"Oh, it's the police." Petal's words automatically have my arm squeezing River's midsection as I pull her closer into me.

All eyes are on me, like the only fucking reason the cops would be at this house would be because of me. Never mind the fact that weed has been going around all fucking night.

When Petal comes back outside, the officers at her heels, her face is ashen and my jaw goes tight at the pained sight of her.

"River, it's for you."

To be continued in The Almost One

https://geni.us/TheAlmostOne

The Blonde One

This book is like the beginning of the end for our girl River. Book 4 of 6! So it's a little bitter-sweet knowing that we're on the home stretch with this series now. But we do get to tie up a lot of ends from the first three in the series, and also fuck shit up a bit and add some more crumbs... because we've still got two books to go after this one... it couldn't all be wrapped up that easily!

As usual, writing with The Brunette One is a freaking blast. Demonstrations of 'moves', trying some things out to see if they work... all while on a zoom call to each other... that's some funny shit right there.

The amount of research we put into each and every book is extensive! From the surroundings, to the food, to the language used—you wouldn't believe the number of times we get stuck in a research hole. We even have an Italian Beta reader, who we wouldn't be without!

Our fabulous editor, David, quit once again... and I'm sure once you've finished this book, you'll know exactly the point that happened! To say he was unhappy is an understatement... but we still love him... and you guys have to trust that even though the ride is bumpy as hell, we'll leave you satisfied in the end ;)

Thank you again to our Betas, our Alpha, our Italian, our David, and our wonderful book-prettifying Lily Wildhart/Sloane Murphy. Y'all rock!

Finally, to the few people that do know me ;) and have been reading these books and feeding back your thoughts... thank you so much for giving these books a chance. I love you all eternally <3

THE BRUNETTE ONE

Holy shitballs, this book was a wild ride to write. I cherish every moment I spend zooming with my Blondie, watching as her man positions her just right to make sure a sex scene is feasible... yeah, you read that right. The sacrifices our better halves make for the sake of art. I love this entire adventure and can't wait to share ALL THE THINGS with you all.

Writing a book, or a series even, isn't something you do all by yourself. We have an entire village–actually the four corners of the world–helping us to make the experience the best it can be for you. From our Italian superwoman (GB, we appreciate you!) to our master formatter, Lily/Sloane to David, our Editing Dom, who doesn't hesitate in using his editing whip to get us back on course, we have our bookworld family helping us.

Then there's you! All of you have given us the fire we need to keep River's story alive. With your inbox messaging, your comments in our reader group, your sharing of our posts and OH MY GOD your fabulous Tik Toks and IG reels. We live for your attention. So thank you, a million times, for allowing us to exist in this little corner of our Romance community.

Words will never be enough to say... you bitches rock!

BOOKS BY N.O. ONE

Dark Contemporary Romance

The Escort Series (MF)

The Rich One ~ https://geni.us/TheRichOne

The Kinky One ~ https://geni.us/TheKinkyOne

The Filthy One ~ https://geni.us/TheFithyOne

The Broken One ~ https://geni.us/TheBrokenOne

The Almost One ~ https://geni.us/TheAlmostOne

The Forever One ~ https://geni.us/TheForeverOne

The Christmas One ~ Prequel to The Escort Series

KOK (RH)

Kings of Kink ~ https://geni.us/KingsOfKink

The Reapers Mafia Crew Duet (MF)

One Kill ~ https://geni.us/TheReapers1

One Love ~ https://geni.us/TheReapers2

The Psycho Trilogy – Sons of Khaos (MF)

Psycho Hate ~ https://geni.us/PsychoHate

Psycho Love ~ https://geni.us/PsychoLove

Psycho Reign ~ https://geni.us/PsychoReign

A Night To Remember Auction (MF)

Fatal

Sons of Khaos – The Standalones

Bear Hunt (MF) ~ https://geni.us/SOKBearHunt

Meat Grinder (Poly with MF and MM)

7 Deadly Sins – A Shared World

Gluttony ~ https://geni.us/SDSGluttony

Next Door

The Assassin Next Door

Dark Paranormal Fantasy Romance

Society Of Soulkeepers

Hack (MF) ~ Book 1 of The White Horse Duet

Hex (MF) ~ Book 2 of The White Horse Duet

If you'd love to get in touch or find out more about our

books, please feel free to stalk us in all the places and join

our newsletter.

www.author-no-one.com

If you'd love to get in touch or find out more about our books, please feel free to stalk us in all the places and join our newsletter.

Here is our linktree: https://linktr.ee/n.o.one

BOOKS WE THINK YOU SHOULD READ

Dark Romance

DATE WITH THE DEVIL (MF) ~
HTTPS://GENI.US/DWTD

Contemporary

THE UCC SAGA
DISHEVELED ~ HTTP://AMZN.TO/2ARPBXP
DISARMED ~ HTTP://AMZN.TO/2MYVXNN
DISCARDED ~ HTTPS://AMZN.TO/2VWTRPF
UCC BOXSET ~ HTTPS://AMZN.TO/3LJVEPE

STANDALONE
THE WISH ~ HTTPS://AMZN.TO/2FTIKQB

Rom-Com

THE WOOLF FAMILY SERIES
SCREWED ~ HTTPS://GENI.US/SCREWED
SCREWED UP ~ HTTPS://BIT.LY/3IBFWKB
SCREWED OVER (COMING SOON)

Supernatural

SOUL GUARDIANS SERIES
REPRISE ~ HTTPS://BIT.LY/3CT9NPE

Eva LeNoir

Fun Flirty Romance

BY LILY WILDHART

Dark Romance

The Saints of Serenity Falls series (RH)
(You will find crossovers from The Escort series by N.O.
One in the Serenity Falls series by Lily Wildhart, and vice
versa!)
A Burn So Deep ~ https://geni.us/burnaltcover
A Revenge So Sweet ~ https://geni.us/revengealtcover
A Taste Of Forever ~ https://geni.us/tastealtcover

Website & Newsletter: www.author-no-one.com

Facebook: https://geni.us/Facebookauthor

Facebook Group: https://geni.us/FierceReaders

Instagram: https://geni.us/Instagramauthor

Goodreads: https://geni.us/Goodreadsauthor

Bookbub: https://www.bookbub.com/profile/n-o-one

Linkedtree https://linktr.ee/n.o.one

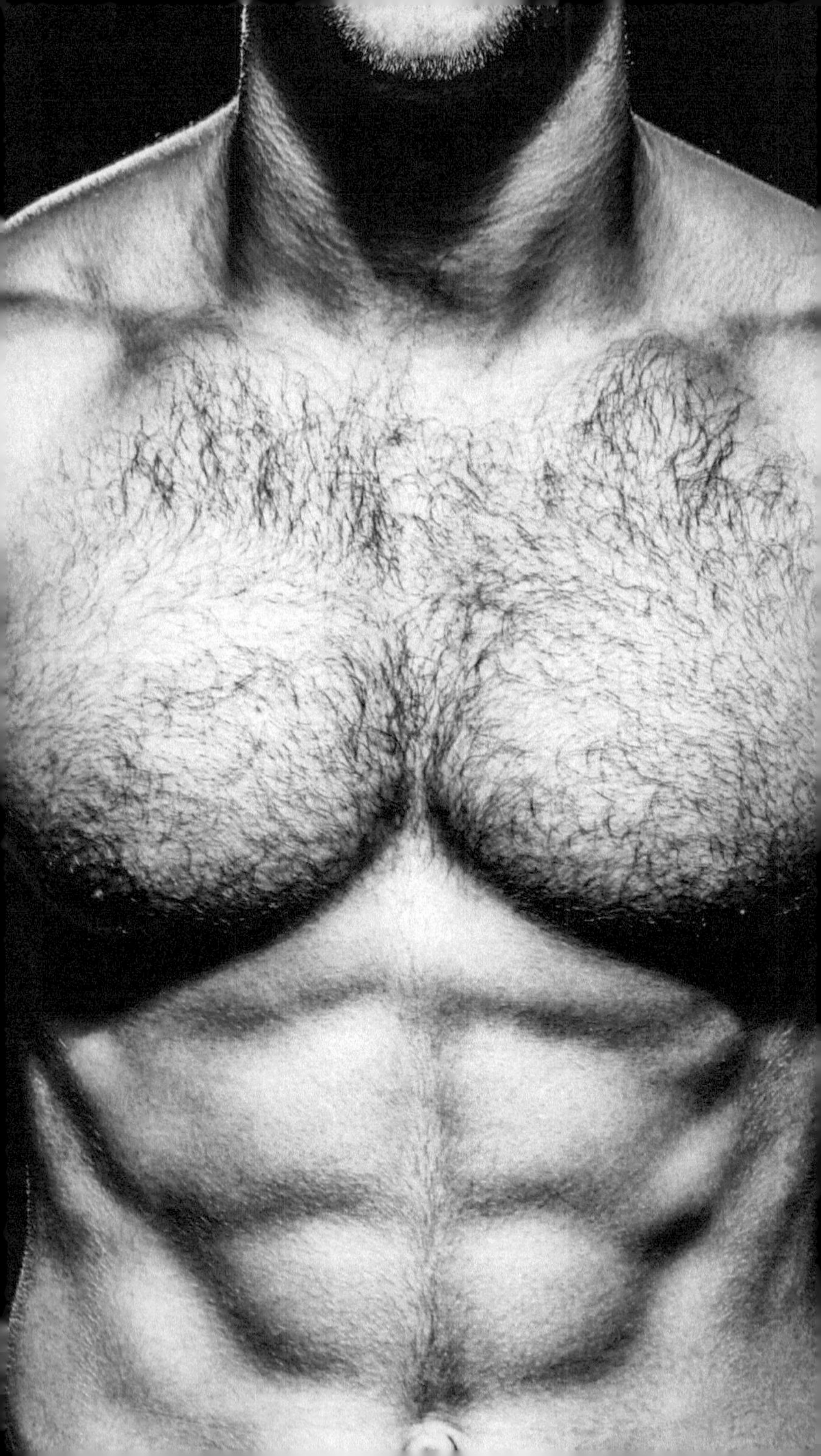